MATCH

A Novel

Kay Day

Rosedale Books

This book is a work of fiction. Names, characters, places, and incidents either are products of the author's imagination or are used fictitiously.

Copyright © 2015 Kay Day

ISBN: 0692575332

For Brent
My true love
My biggest fan

MATCH

1

Bird poop misses my thumb by like half an inch. Right there on the handlebar of my bike. It's purple—the splat, not my bike. My bike is black. Wonder what that bird's been eating.

I peer into the branches above me and spot a magpie. He squawks at me and flies away. Dude. I use a leaf to wipe the poop off. If I were a girl I'd probably have a lilac scented tissue or something. But the leaf does the job.

The street is clear so I pedal across to Lake

View Rest Home. It used to be called The Old Miner's Home, which actually made sense because it was founded for old miners. Mountain View would make sense. This town is surrounded by mountains. We're like, nine thousand feet up in the Colorado Rockies for Pete's sake. But Lake View? There's no lake for like ten miles.

Whatever.

I lean my bike against the chain link fence. Mrs. Holmes yells at me from her house next door. "Good morning, Mark."

My name's not Mark.

I've been called a lot of names in my life. MacGillicuddy. Mac. Copper top. Red. Freckles. Matthew, which actually is my name. Grandma calls me Sparky and Grandpa called me Nuisance. But the name I can't get rid of is Matt the Matchstick. Or usually, just Match.

I really do look like a dumb matchstick. A knobby one. With big feet. I'm the tallest fourteen-year-old around and it's more obvious because of my beacon of a head.

I say good morning to Mrs. Holmes and then walk toward the nursing home before she can send me on some errand. She'll keep me busy all summer if I let her.

"Mark...Mark...Mark!" she says. But I pretend I don't hear her and walk faster.

It's a creepy stone building. Not very big, but still creepy. The inside isn't as old as the outside. But still really old. I think they updated in, like, the eighties. The tops of the walls have a strip of wallpaper with geese on it. I'm not kidding. Geese.

My nose wrinkles as I go in the front door. It usually smells kinda like meatloaf no matter what time of day.

You may wonder what I'm doing here. This is where my mom used to work and I had to hang out with her after school because she didn't want me at home getting in Dad's way. It got so's I made friends with one of the residents and now, even though I don't have to, I like to come visit him. Mr. Mac is kinda like a substitute grandpa or something, you know?

I go to the nurses' desk and see Liz doing some paperwork. She's my favorite. Her hair is purple with pink stripes. And she's like, at least thirty.

"Hi, Matt!" She actually uses my real name, usually.

"Hi, Liz. Where's Mr. Mac?"

"Parlor."

"Thanks!" I wave and she winks at me.

Awkward, but she's like that.

I go down the hall, my shoes squeaking on the white linoleum, and say hi to people along the way. A few feet from the door to the parlor, my left foot goes straight out from under me. It shoots up in front and takes the other foot with it. Bam! Right on my rear.

"Oh dear! Oh honey, are you all right? Oh, Frank, go get the nurse, quick. This boy needs help." A woman with a crooked wig peers down at me from her wheelchair, and a man hobbles away with his walker toward the nurses' desk hollering, "Nurse! Nurse!"

I grab the handrail that runs along the wall and pull myself up. My face is burning. So's my rear end.

"I'm OK. Really. I'm all right," I say as I ease toward the doorway.

She wheels along beside me. "Are you sure, honey? Maybe you should wait for the nurse?"

"I'm OK. Really."

Liz comes around the corner, "What's going on? Is someone hurt?"

"Oh goodness, this young man fell down flat."

Liz looks at me and raises an eyebrow. "Are you all right?"

My face feels hot. "Yes. I'm all right, for Pete's sake!"

She covers her mouth so I won't see her laughing.

"It's the stupid slick floors," I say.

"Yet you seem to be the only one who ever falls around here." She pats my back and walks away.

The wheelchair lady pats my hand and then

follows after Liz. "Don't you think he should see a doctor?"

The parlor is a large room trying to look homey with couches and chairs scattered around in groups. Several residents sit around reading books, watching TV, or just staring out the window. Mr. Mac is watching the birds they have. Parakeets.

"Hi," I say.

"WELL, HI THERE LITTLE MAC!"

I cringe and try not to back away. Wish I'd remembered my stupid earplugs.

I look at the birds. Some are blue and some are yellow. They have smashed-in faces.

"HOW ARE THE GIRLS TREATING YOU?"

"They leave me alone, Mr. Mac, and I'm glad."

"OH, I SUPPOSE SO. ONE OF THESE DAYS,

THOUGH…" He slugs me on the shoulder.

Yeah, right. That's what everyone says, but I don't know how a guy can even talk to girls. I used to have girls for friends, but well… it got… weird.

"LET'S GO FOR A WALK." We go out the double doors into a little park-type area with concrete paths, birdbaths, and log benches. There are lots of old trees so the place is nice and shady. Probably a lot of dumb birds in the trees, too.

At the first bench he sits down and I sit next to him. That's what he means by a walk.

"HERE YOU GO." He hands me a butterscotch candy from his pocket.

"Thank you."

You know, the guy isn't even hard of hearing. Maybe he thinks everyone else is. Or maybe he's always talked like an air-horn.

We suck on our candies and sit there. This is what we do. I like him because he doesn't ask me a bunch of questions like most people. How's school? How's your summer? All that stuff. A guy gets tired of that, you know?

Mr. Mac rests his elbows on his knees and his head in his hands.

"Is something wrong?" I ask.

He looks up at me, his eyes are rimmed with pink and they look wet and mushy.

"I haven't heard from my son for two weeks."

The first time I've heard him speak without yelling.

"You usually hear from him every few days, don't you?"

"Yep. Mostly asking for money or something. The boy's a rascal and always up to no good. Still,

I hear from him regularly. I even tried calling him, but no answer."

My ears itch. My heart starts beating a little faster.

He swipes a fly off his pant leg. "I called the sheriff, said he's not been seen lately but she hasn't figured anything out yet."

I swallow too loud.

"I'd hate something to have happened to him," Mr. Mac says.

My heart goes up another notch, "What do you think happened?"

"Who knows?" He swipes at the fly again. "Could be anything I guess. I don't know what that boy's up to. Weird for him to just disappear like that, though."

I try to swallow a lump and my hand flaps against my thigh like a dying fish.

Mr. Mac looks at me a second and then puts his arm across my shoulder. I wish he hadn't done that. I ain't gonna cry, darn it.

I know what it's like to have someone go missing.

We sit quietly a minute while I force the tears back down. He's probably thinking about my mom, too. He always told me he wished she was his daughter.

Mr. Mac moves his arm and clears his throat. "Stan's always getting into trouble. Maybe he finally messed with the wrong people."

Maybe, but he probably just took off. Didn't care about anyone else and took off. That's what a jerk like him would do, I bet.

2

When I come out of the nursing home I pull a slip of paper out of my pocket. I got it memorized, but I read it anyway.

"Hey, Mark!" Mrs. Holmes says. She's still on her porch, nearly hidden by all the plants out there.

I fold the paper carefully and put it back in my pocket.

She always calls me Mark and no matter how many times I tell her my name she just doesn't get it. Drives me nuts. I finally gave up trying to correct her.

I walk over to her gate. "Hello, Mrs. Holmes."

She waves me toward her, "Come on up here. Don't be a butt."

I smell cinnamon so I open the gate. It's crooked and I have to lift it to get it open. The sidewalk is all uneven from the tree roots or something. I have to watch my step.

Mrs. Holmes is very tall for an old woman and she wears her white hair up fancy like that lady in *The Birds*. You know, that old movie where crows kill people? Anyway, someone told me she used to be a model or something. She dresses real fancy, but today her clothes are on wrong-side out. I won't say anything, though. I did once and she called me something worse than a butt.

A brown creature drops from the ceiling onto my shoulder—her squirrel monkey.

My heart pounds and I freeze.

He looks at me with his tiny black eyes.

His teeth are inches from my nose.

I close my eyes.

All I can hear is my heart thumping and a weird buzzing sound.

Creepy little monkey feet cling to my arm.

Creepy little monkey fingers pull on my ear.

The floor feels slanted.

Mrs. Holmes' voice breaks through the buzzing, "Mark…Mark… Oh for heaven's sake."

The monkey lifts from my shoulder, trying to take my shirt with him.

I open my eyes. Mrs. Holmes puts him on a rocking chair.

I let out my breath.

Dude. One of these days that crazy monkey is going to take a bite of me; I just know it. If I didn't smell that cinnamon wafting through the door, I'd be out of here.

I settle my breathing and try to look like I didn't just act like a scaredy-cat baby.

She spreads her arms wide and takes a deep breath. "Isn't this day just full of fruity goodness, Mark?"

I take a big sniff. Maybe she's making some kind of fruit cookies this time, but I can't tell.

"I don't know," I say.

"Oh of course it is."

She hands me a box with eight potted plants in it. "I want you to take these to the park for me."

Mr. Nutsy crawls over to pick at a leaf.

"Um, why?" I take the box from her, keeping my eye on that monkey.

"Because they need a change of scenery. This is a perfect day for them to sit out in the park amongst some shrubbery they haven't met before."

"I don't get it."

She peers into my eyes, "Do you really think you have to understand everything, Mark?"

I just look at her. Never going to understand *her*, that's for sure.

"All right, be off." She grabs Mr. Nutsy and puts him on her head. "Make sure you put them amongst some nice shrubbery! No riffraff."

"Do you want me to leave them there?"

"Land sakes, no! What are you thinking? You can't abandon them. You must return them home after they are finished."

Finished what? I don't want to ask, so I just turn and walk toward the park. The park is two blocks north. Mrs. Holmes won't travel any further north than her house. She says the gravitational pull will overtake her. Luckily, the grocery store and the diner are both south.

I've taken dogs for walks before, but never plants. Was this like a play date or something?

I'm half way to the park when Emma and Ann come around the corner. They're in my class at school and at church.

"Hey, Match," Emma says.

I start to walk around them, but Emma blocks my way.

"Match?"

My heart thumps, "Hi, Emma." My voice squeaks. I am so lame.

She looks into the box, "What have you got there?"

"Um, just some plants."

The gold in her hair glints in the sun.

She looks at me with questions in her eyes. Her big brown eyes, like warm chocolate.

I feel my face burn. Great, now I'm really lame.

"Uh, I gotta go." I scoot around her and move down the sidewalk. I hear Ann giggle and Emma say, "Shut up."

At the corner I turn around and watch her walk away.

Dude.

3

I stash the box of plants under a bush. Not riffraff shrubbery, I hope. I hear someone behind me and turn around.

It's Bean. He got his nickname cause he stuck a bean in his ear once when we were nine. That's supposed to be a secret, though. He thinks most people think it's because his name is Ben. But see, when I was nine, I wasn't a very good secret keeper. I'm sure people know the whole story.

"Hey man, what's happenin'?" He always

watches old '60s and '70s movies and now he likes to talk like a hippie or something all the time. Drives me nuts.

He doesn't look like a hippie, though. His brown hair's about half an inch long. He calls it a Buzzard Cut.

"Mrs. Holmes' plants are having a play date." I tell him about her crazy request.

He looks at the plants and shakes his head. "I usually just go to the Milky Way for some ice cream when she sends me on some weird errand and she never knows the difference."

We walk around the park looking for something to do. The old swings and merry-go-round remind me of when I was a kid. My dad says they're the same ones he played on.

Over by the pond we see some old hamburgers lying on a picnic table. They are all dried out and flies are all over them. A squirrel runs off with a piece and eats it under a tree. Dude, I didn't know squirrels ate meat.

"Why would people abandon hamburgers? That's insane," I say.

Bean picks one up and inspects it. He peels one of the buns off.

"Ew, gross," he throws the hamburger against the bathroom wall. It lands condiment side and sticks.

Mom and Dad used to get us burgers and we'd come and sit at this same table. Now that it's just Dad and me we don't do that anymore.

"Dude." I grab another hamburger, pull off the bun and lob it at the wall. Stupid burger.

I reach for the last one but Bean grabs it before I can. It takes two tries for it to stick.

I find a bunch of ketchup packets in a bag

and so I dump them out. I fold one in half on the ground and stomp on it. The ketchup squirts across the concrete. I take another and do it again. Stupid ketchup.

"Hey, give me a chance." Bean grabs one and puts it next to mine. His doesn't shoot as far. "Man."

We each grab another and stomp at the same time. This time he wins. But I don't care, I just keep stomping.

After we squish all the packets, I decide Mrs. Holmes' plants have probably been out long enough.

I go over and get the box.

Wait...

"Hey, weren't there eight plants?" I look at the seven in the box.

"How would I know, man?" Bean's standing

behind me trying to blow a folded leaf like a whistle.

"Dude. There were eight. Where is the other one?"

We both look around the shrubbery but can't find the other plant.

"You probably just counted wrong," he says.

"I didn't count wrong."

"Why would you even count them in the first place?"

"I don't know, I just did, all right? And there were eight. Four and four. Eight."

"Well, how could one be missing? I mean we could see the whole time and nobody's been over here."

"I don't know."

"Man, I think you're freaking or something. Let's just take them back. You'll see. There were only seven."

"Dang it, Bean. There were not."

This ain't good. She's not going to be happy. Hope she doesn't sic that monkey on me.

As we walk toward the sidewalk I see The Old Guy Who Lives in the Park waving at us from a bench. He doesn't know his name or where he came from or nothing. He's got amnesia. Bean calls it ambrosia. We usually just call him The Old Guy for short.

He just showed up here when I was about four. He was wearing torn clothing and kinda beat up. People tried to get him to go to Denver or somewhere to a shelter or something, but he won't leave the park. Hasn't once in ten years.

"How are you boys today?"

"We're fine. Hey, did you see anyone over there by those bushes?"

"Nope. I haven't seen anyone but you and me. Why?"

He looks like a college professor or something. Dresses nice, in clothes that people have donated to him. Seems like he probably went to college, too. Not the kind of guy you expect to live in a park.

"One of these plants disappeared."

He looks into the cardboard box, "What are you doing with these?"

"Just doing a favor for someone."

"Hmmm. I didn't see anything. Are you sure one is missing?"

"Yeah. I'm sure," I say and roll my eyes at Bean. Does everyone think I'm four or something? I can count to eight.

"If you say so. I'll keep my eye out for it. Maybe it's still around here somewhere."

"Okay, thanks," I say and we turn back to the sidewalk.

Bean goes with me back to Mrs. Holmes'.

"Mark! Bob! Come on up boys." She has some cookies and milk waiting for us. I guess she knew that when cookies are involved Bean will probably show up.

"Did they have a good time?" She asks as she peers into the box.

"As far as I could tell."

"Oh no! Binky! Where's Binky?"

She moves the plants around and then looks under the box.

"I… uh…."

"Those rotten Boogonians!" She shakes her fist and looks, like, really mad.

Bean and I look at each other and both mouth "Boogonians?"

"I'm sorry, Mrs. Holmes," I say. "I didn't see anyone. There wasn't anything I could do."

"I know, boy." She pats my head. "There never is when it comes to those savages."

She takes the box into the house and closes the door without another word.

We sit on the porch enjoying the cookies, because even if the lady is a psycho, she sure can bake.

Bean pulls a packet of ketchup from his pocket and swirls some onto his snicker-doodle. When he gets it just right he takes a bite. "Mmm…." He sighs and rolls his eyes back into his head.

People are weird. No doubt about that.

4

I stop at the mailbox when I get home. Awesome! The DVD arrived. Star Wars. The first one—the *real* first one. This has been on our queue, like, forever. I'm gonna watch it right now.

We don't get TV reception or cable up here so I live for the red envelopes in the mail. Especially when it's one of my choices and not one of Dad's lame westerns or cop shows.

I pedal up our long driveway, staying to the side because it's smoother than the thick gravel.

Dad's out in the barn mucking out stalls. He always talks a lot while he works. He talks to himself, the horses, the walls, whatever.

"Come on over here, consarn it you little turd. You ain't gettin' away from me."

Oh. So now he's talking to horse poop.

You know Yosemite Sam, that short guy in the Bugs Bunny cartoon? With the big mustache? That's what my dad looks like. Talks like him, too.

"Matthew!"

Dang it. He saw me.

"Come on, Son, give me a hand with this."

Why does everyone always have something for me to do? I lean my bike against a tree, put the mail on the porch, and trudge to the barn.

"Where's Ron and Ray?" I ask. They're our ranch hands.

"Ray's out exercising the horses. And Ron

ran to the Big R."

Nobody rides quite like Ray does. I gotta go see.

I run out to the pasture fence.

About two years ago he started wearing a cape all the time. At first the horses were scared spitless. But he figured horses had to get used to capes in the old days so these horses could too. And they did. Now they're less skittish in general, thanks to his cape therapy.

He's tearing across the pasture at full gallop, cape flying behind him, shouting, "I'll chase him 'round the moons of Nibia and 'round the Antares Maelstrom and 'round Perdition's flames before I give him up!"

He calls himself a Trekker. Whatever. But he's sure good with the horses.

"Matthew!" Dad hollers.

"Coming…"

"Start over there," Dad says when I get inside the barn.

I start in the stall across from him, scooping manure and straw into a wheelbarrow. I'll get it done really fast, then I can go in and watch that movie. I gotta start watching it before Dad gets in the house because he'll want to watch Rockford Files or something. But if I've already started my movie, he'll let me finish.

I grab the shovel and start scooping. I love everything about horses but this.

Dad starts talking to stuff again. "Get out of the way. Who put you there anyway?"

I don't bother to look. He could be talking to a bag of grain, a rope, a bucket, anything really. Drives me nuts. I start shoveling faster.

"Hey, slow down there, Son. Do it right."

Darn.

He goes on with his one-way conversation. I can't take it anymore. Gotta think of something to talk about.

Wait, I know. "Hey, Dad…"

"Huh?"

"You know that guy, Stan?"

He stops and looks at me. "Yeah. What about him?"

"I guess he's…" my throat feels weird. "His dad hasn't heard from him. He doesn't know where he is."

I keep shoveling.

"That's too bad. For his dad, I mean. The rest of us are probably better off without the blasted son of a gun."

"I know, right?"

My stall is finished. "All done, can I go in

now?"

"Dagnabbit, boy, do the next one."

Darn.

I move to the next stall. He ain't gonna let me out of here, I know it.

He starts talking to his shovel.

I interrupt him. "A few weeks ago I was riding my bike down Main Street, minding my own business, you know, totally off the road and everything. Stan drove by and, like, laid on the horn and yelled out his window and threw an apple core at me. Almost made me wreck."

"Dadblamed fool."

"I heard he poisoned someone's dog one time."

"Well, I don't know, but I wouldn't put it past him."

I finish this stall, and look at the next four.

Shoot. I sigh and move on to the next.

"So, Dad, what do you think happened to him?" My heart pounds just thinking about it. When I asked him this question about Mom he blew me off. Told me I didn't need to worry about it. That the authorities would take care of it and that I should go take a bath. He treats me like I'm four or something.

"Maybe he lit out. Or maybe someone figured out how to run him out."

Lit out. I wonder if that's what he thinks Mom did.

"Or maybe he's dead." I say.

He stops scooping and looks at me a minute, his face sad.

"Well, someone could have killed him or something, you know." I look down at the manure pile in front of me.

Mom could be dead. Nobody would ever want to kill her, but maybe she had an accident.

"I don't know about that. But I reckon some people probably would like to."

I try to keep my focus on Stan.

"Especially if he poisoned their dog."

"Or worse."

"He's done worse?"

"From what I've heard."

"Dude. Like what?"

"It's all just rumors. We don't need to be talking about it." He returns to his conversation with his environment.

There he goes again. Blowing me off. Guess I'll have to get the answer somewhere else.

I work faster, ignoring Dad's jabbering. I wonder what Stan did?

I quickly finish my row of stalls and stick the

shovel in the corner. I'm faster than him because he's old. "I'm going in now."

"Wait a minute. You can't leave them like that."

"What's wrong with them?"

"You did a half-way job. You know that when I ask you to do something I expect you to do the thing right. Get that push-broom and get the rest of that crud out of there."

Shoot! They look fine to me.

I kick the wall and grab the broom. I'm never going to get to watch Star Wars now.

Maybe if I sweep really fast.

"When you're done with that, I want you to help me clean out the feed troughs."

Darn.

5

A few days later I go back to see Mr. Mac and manage to get to his room without kissing the linoleum. And this time I remembered earplugs. I shove them in and sit on the edge of his bed.

He's sitting in a recliner next to me. "Hey there, Little Mac." He slugs me on the arm. "How are the girls treating you."

I don't give him my usual answer. "Find out anything about your son?" I ask instead.

He shakes his head. "The sheriff says she

ain't heard anything. Figures he just went out of town for a while. I guess that's possible, but it don't seem right to me. Wish I weren't stuck in this place so I could be of some use."

I bet she kinda hopes the guy never shows up again. I wouldn't mind either. Except…well, it's just wrong to not know where somebody is.

Mr. Mac's forehead's all wrinkled up in that worried way adults get. "You think you could check around?" he looks at me. "Maybe ask some questions?" His wet eyes search mine.

Dude. I can't. Really. I'm sure everyone in town is glad to be rid of Stan and I'm supposed to go around asking what happened to him? Besides, I really just want to forget about this business.

"Umm… I don't think I can right now. I…I'm really busy this summer. And… uh…"

"No, no it's OK. Never mind. Not your

problem anyway. I shouldn't have asked."

I can see the disappointment on his face. I feel like a total loser.

I stop by Bonnie's Beauty Emporium on the way home. Bean's sweeping up a wad of hair.

"Dude, what are you doing?" I say.

He puts the broom away and we walk outside.

"Mom told me I have to help today. She said she'd pay me, man." He grins like that's the best news he's ever heard. Bean loves money.

We sit out on a bench along the sidewalk. Tourists surge by carrying bags of t-shirts and fudge. Claimsville isn't a main destination. We're just a stop on the way to bigger and better places. But it's pretty here, so the streets are crowded from May through August.

"What's happenin'?" Bean says.

"Wanna go camping tomorrow?"

"Yeah, man! That'd be far out. I'll ask Mom. She'll let me. I'm irritating her today, I can tell. " He grins.

I laugh. He's got a good mom, but his weird habits drive her nuts.

"Let's stay the whole night this time, OK?" I say.

"Oh man, definitely. I wanted to last time but you wanted to go home."

"Liar." I shove him because that is not the truth at all. We both wanted to go home.

He shoves me back, "Wimp."

"My dad will probably bring that up, you know? I hope he doesn't use it as a reason to say no."

"Yeah, but we are way older now. No way are we going to chicken out this time."

"Of course, not. But will he believe that?"

Bean shrugs. "Call me after you talk to him."

"Cool."

◆ ◆ ◆

Dad comes in from running some errands, slams the door and stomps over to his chair. "Dad-blame them good-for-nothing fancy-pants!" He takes off his boots and throws them across the room.

"What's the deal, Dad?" I look at the mud smear on the wall where his boots hit. I'd never get away with doing something like that.

"Those yahoos at the garage told me that my truck can't be fixed. Said she's an eyesore anyway and that I should just junk her. That pickup has been in this valley since before most of them was born, consarn it. She has a lot of years in her yet."

I try not to laugh. Dad loves me, he loves his

land, but he would trade me and the land both for that pick-up, I think. Roxanne, he calls her. My dad learned to drive in it and everything. She's a good ol' truck, for sure, but she is old and she is ug-a-ly.

"Take it to a shop in Denver, Dad."

"Oh, you can count on it. Just 'cause she don't start all the times I want her to don't mean she's done."

A few weeks ago somebody bashed in the front of Roxanne. You should have seen Dad then. The headlights and grill were broken and ruined. Nobody else can even tell the difference, but Dad was mad as a kid with homework on Christmas. Said he'd find out who did it and he'd make him pay.

He likes to yell, but usually that's it. I'd never seen him hurt anyone, except there was a rumor that he beat up a guy once. The guy called him Yosemite. I already told you he looks like him. Doesn't much like the comparison, though, I guess.

After eating a bowl of chili, Dad settles down in front of the TV. Now that he's cozy watching an old cop show he's in a better mood.

"Dad, Bean and I want to go camping tomorrow night. Is that OK?

He looks at me a minute. "You've got chores."

"I can do them first. I'll get up early."

"It didn't work out so well last summer."

I knew it. "I know, but…"

"You guys going to come home in the middle of the night, crying and pitchin' fits 'cause you're scared."

"Dad. Last year we were younger. And we

weren't crying."

"Looked like crying to me. The horses were in a state. It's a wonder you hadn't broken one of their legs or one of your necks rushing down the mountain in pitch dark, like that."

He's said all this before. Several times.

"I know. I know," I say. "But we won't do that this year. We're in High school now, for Pete's sake."

He smirks a little and nods. "All right. See that those chores are done first."

"Cool. I'll call him now."

Bean answers on the first ring.

"Dude, Dad says we can go. What about your mom?"

"She thinks it's a great idea."

"Awesome! So, I've got hotdogs and pop. Can you bring the Twinkies?"

"Yep. I've already got a couple of boxes under my bed. I'll bring extra garlic powder, too, in case you want some."

"Dude, I am never, ever putting garlic on my Twinkies."

"You don't know what you're missing," he says.

Gag.

"So your mom will bring you before she goes to work?" I say.

"Yep. I'll be there about 9:30."

"Cool. See ya then."

I hang up and join Dad watching The Rockford Files he got on DVD. I usually get Psych or cool movies. Mom usually got something mushy. But she also watched sci-fi with me. Dad won't have anything to do with aliens and all that. I look at the empty spot on the couch. Mom's favorite pillow looks lonely. The old table next to the couch still has the coaster where she kept her cup of tea.

The room is too empty. I can't stand it.

I get up. "I'm going to bed," I say, and go to my room before Dad can ask why I'm turning in at 9:00.

6

The next morning I rush through my chores. Living on a ranch is a lot of work. Even though we've got Ron and Ray, Dad still makes me work. Says it's good for me. Whatever.

After I give the horses some oats and fill up their water troughs, I run inside to pack up my bag.

Bean's mom drops him off and waves at me before she leaves in a swirl of red dust. His tan face has a big ol grin on it.

In the barn we toss our stuff in a corner and

grab bridles and saddles. I open the stall and my horse, Julie, has a t-shirt on. Seriously. A t-shirt. It's like one of those dog shirts only much bigger. And it says, "I heart Match."

Dude, really?

Bean has a fit behind me. He's snorting and rolling around on the floor.

Ron stands in a corner snickering. He always tries to pretend he's all innocent. He is anything but innocent.

My dad comes out carrying a camera.

"All right, Son, go put your arm around her and smile."

I just look at him.

"You boys ain't leaving until I get a dadblamed photo, so you may as well do it."

Darn it.

I put my arm over her neck and show my

teeth.

"Give her a kiss," Bean squawks between giggles.

"That's the way, boy. Now when you get a girlfriend I can give her a copy."

"Dad! Dude."

Bean still squirms on the floor. Dad slaps himself on the leg and Ron still snickers.

I reach up and undo the Velcro on the back of the shirt. "Come help me get this off, Ron. You put it on her."

He comes and helps me undo the rest of the Velcro to get it off her legs. He looks too proud of himself.

My face burns while I saddle her up. Bean snorts every now and then as he gets his horse ready. Finally, we're mounted up and ready to go.

I holler for Wilma. She's a good camping dog.

She's about knee high and round, but hard, not fat. Her hair is short and rough and the color of dirt. She can tear a tire off a truck with her teeth. She could have someone's leg chomped up to his knee before he even had time to scream. We like her.

Dad comes over and checks the cinches on our saddles, as if I don't know what I'm doing.

"Be sure you tie them up well."

I sigh. "We will, Dad."

"Give them access to plenty of grass and fresh water."

"Geez, Dad, I know what to do."

He grins at me. "Don't come home crying in the middle of the night."

I roll my eyes. "We won't, Dad."

He smacks my horse on the rump. "Have fun then."

We wave as we ride off. He waves back and then saunters toward his truck. That's something my dad does. Saunter. It's a cowboy thing.

We're going to a spot not far off the trail behind our house, so we don't have to worry too much about wild things getting us. Crazy hook-handed murderers, though? That we need to worry about.

Bean starts in with an old cowboy song, "Back in the saddle again..." Singing cowboy songs is a tradition we started last year. I join in, belting out the tune the best I can, which ain't good.

We round a bend and I recognize the place where we get off the trail. I rein Julie over and we enter a grove of aspen. The rustle of the leaves always makes me think of Mom. She loves that sound. Or she did...or...does?

Bean's horse is Gary. All our horses have people names. That was my dad's idea. The people who used to go on trail rides thought it was weird so sometimes I told them their horse was named Trigger or something, just to ease their minds. We aren't doing trail rides this summer. Dad says he isn't up to it. It was usually Mom's job.

There's a small meadow with a stream running alongside. We hop off and take care of the horses. Then we open our packs and dig out the cheese puffs and root beer. After we've had a bunch of junk, we get our sandwiches and eat those, too. Then the Twinkies. This is the life.

After we build a fire ring and gather some wood, we walk over to the stream and toss in some rocks. We follow along to see where it takes us, sometimes stopping to see who can make the biggest splash.

There's still snow in the shady spots. It's grainy from being around so long. I pick some up and throw it at Bean, but it falls like sand and misses by a foot.

I turn to get some more but get my shirt hung up on a bush.

"Stupid," I say as I inspect my shirt for holes. My mom gave me this shirt. All right, so she gave me all my shirts, so what?

"That bush is probably 'riffraff.'" Beans says and laughs.

I laugh thinking about my dumb plant errand.

"Still drives me nuts wondering what happened to that plant." I say.

"Really man? Let it go already. It's just a plant."

"But it just vanished. Don't you want to know what happened to it?"

"Not really. I don't even think about it. You think too much. You'll give yourself a tumor or something."

Oh brother.

We walk on, me thinking, and him avoiding a tumor. How do you not think, anyway?

About a mile up we smell something. We both stand there with our noses in the air. Wilma whines and then she crouches with her tail between her legs. Bean and I look at her and shrug.

"Man, what's up with your dog? She's kinda freaking out."

"I don't know, dude. Must be the smell."

We sniff some more.

"Smells like...root beer?" Bean says.

"Not exactly. Like… burnt root beer?"

"Burnt root beer with…mustard?"

We shrug again and keep walking. You never know what people do up here. Maybe someone burnt some root beer and mustard.

Wilma skulks along behind us like she's been whacked with a newspaper or something. She's usually such a tough dog, not afraid of anything. My heart rate speeds up a little.

The scent grows stronger. I stop.

"Dude, do you hear anything?"

Bean tilts his head a little. "No man. You?"

"No. That's the point. Usually there's jays and crows making some kind of racket. I don't hear anything."

Goose bumps pop up on my arms.

In front of us is a dense clump of pine trees.

"What do you think?" I ask. "Should we, like,

go in there?"

Bean's face is kinda ghost-ish. He looks at Wilma and then at the trees. "I don't know man. I mean, I would, but we don't want to scare your dog."

Yeah, right.

The pattering in my chest makes me want to get out of here, too. "Yeah, maybe we should, like, take her back to camp."

"Yeah, man. Maybe we should."

We look at each other for a minute before we move on. I know he's just as curious as I am to find the answer to this.

I go into the dark, cool stand of pine and he follows. All we see is trees. But up ahead the forest opens up again so we head toward the light.

Makes me think of when they joke on TV about going toward the light when someone is dying. Not a good thought to have right now.

When we get into the open we see that all the trees are broken. Just in one area, about the size of a city block. Looks like a tornado set down and lifted back up.

The burnt-root-beer odor is really intense. Weird that broken trees would smell like that. You'd think they'd smell like pine. But it's definitely them causing the stink.

We walk to the nearest tree. It isn't broken. It's bent. How do you bend a tree? Bean and I stare. His mouth is hanging open. I guess mine is too. They're all bent. Hundreds maybe.

Wilma is crazy, barking and snarling and running around in circles. The fur on her back is sticking straight up.

"Let's go up there and get a better look." I point to a small rise on the other side of the smashed trees.

When we get to the top we turn to look and I can't believe my eyes. It is a circle. A crop circle made of pine trees!

I barely hear Bean say, "Far out."

We sit on a boulder and I try to breathe. My throat feels kinda closed off and my heart won't settle down.

We sit for a long time, neither of us saying a thing. Bean's mouth is still hanging open. I can't even think.

I trace the pattern over and over again with my eyes. Around and around. A perfect circle. The trees kinda woven over each other.

"These things are hoaxes, right?" Bean says, making me jump. "I mean, some guys with boards on their feet make 'em, don't they?"

"But... But these are trees. These are two or

three-foot diameter pines. Who could have stomped on them?" I say.

Bean shakes his head and shrugs. "Bigfoot?"

"Yeah. I don't think even Bigfoot's feet are that big."

We shuffle back to camp. Bean kicks a pinecone and I nearly jump out of my skin.

A tree circle. I never heard of such a thing. My heart thumps too loud. Bean is looking around with eyes wide like someone is going to grab him at any minute.

Back at camp we sit on our sleeping bags and dig through our packs for chips and Cokes.

The horses graze quietly. The odor doesn't seem to reach over here. Wilma is curled up next to me, but her eyes are watchful.

Truth is I want to go home. I look at Bean. He fidgets and looks uncomfortable. No way I'm telling him I'm scared. No way he's gonna tell me, either. And no way can we give my dad the satisfaction. We wouldn't get to go camping again until we're eighteen.

So, I grab my fishing pole and walk to the creek. Bean grabs his and follows. We each cast off and find a place to sit on the bank.

"So, I got a new game, did I tell you?" Bean says.

"I don't think so. Which one?"

"It's that first-person alien shooter I was telling you about."

"Oh yeah. Cool."

We keep on talking about anything we can think of besides what's really on our minds. I'm just not ready and I guess Bean feels the same way.

I catch a couple of sweet trout. Bean only catches one, but his is bigger. We clean them and get a fire going. We didn't bring a pan so we put our fish on sticks like hot dogs. But they taste way better than hot dogs.

The sun sets and we savor some Twinkies for dessert. We finally start saying the words that have been whirling in our minds.

"What could have done that?" Bean asks. I don't ask what he's talking about. I know he isn't talking about the foul odor floating through the campsite. We both know he did that.

"I don't know," I say.

"Aliens?" he says.

I look at him. I had never thought aliens could be real—until now.

I shrug.

"Something really big," he says. "Bigger than Bigfoot."

"It's the freakiest thing I've seen in my life." I

poke the coals with a stick and toss on another log. I'm not letting this fire go out, that's for sure.

"Man, the press is going to dig this."

"We can't tell the press, dude."

"We have to. We can't just keep it to ourselves."

I look at him. "Why not?"

"Because, man, it's way too big. We're just a couple of kids. This is huge."

"It's not like we have to do anything about it. Seriously, if people hear about this, it will totally mess things up around here."

"How's it going to mess things up? Besides, we'll get our names in the paper! And probably our pictures too, man. That would be groovy. We'll be famous."

"If this gets out, the place will be full of crazies. All those hippie, earthy, new-age people will invade our town to worship the tree gods or aliens or whatever. We don't need nuts crawling all over, messing up our woods. Selling crystals in the shops. We can't say a word."

"Man…"

"Is it worth all that just to get your picture in the paper? We wouldn't even be able to come up here without running into a bunch of people. Nothing would be the same. You know?"

He picks at the mud on his shoe with a stick. "All right. I guess you got a point."

"You better promise."

"Yeah. I promise."

That night we don't tell ghost stories like we planned. I lie awake looking at the stars. What in the world happened to those trees? There has to be a good explanation, right?

Something snaps in the trees and I sit up.

Bean sits up, too. It's just the horses.

"You still awake?" Bean said.

"Yep."

"Me, too."

We lay back down.

"Do you think it's safe here, man?" Bean says. "I mean, your dad may not want us to come home in the middle of the night, but don't you think he'd rather us do that than get killed by giant tree-benders?"

"There aren't any giant tree-benders, dude."

"Oh, right. Those trees are just lying down to take a nap."

"Well… the tree benders aren't going to kill us." I hope.

Every little noise wakes me with a startle. The ground never seemed so hard. The night never seemed so long.

When we wake up we eat our donuts and pack up the horses. We will be home much earlier than we planned, but Dad will be out in the pasture so he won't ask any questions.

7

Ron and Ray Roy are at the barn when we arrive. Yeah, their last name is Roy. They can unpack for us. I'm beat.

Bean and I leave the horses with them and go into the house for a drink. Bean calls his mom and then we sit in front of the TV.

Dad stomps in the back door, knocking manure and junk off his boots onto the mat.

"Well, Son, how are the horses?"

"They're fine, Dad." I smile. Some people

would be jealous, but Mom told me that "horses" really means me.

"You boys have a good time?"

"Yep."

"Get scared?"

Bean and I look at each other. He wants to say something, I can tell. I shake my head at him.

"No sir," Bean says.

"We stuck it out, Dad, just like I said we would."

"Good." He goes in the kitchen and opens the fridge.

"Remember. No telling." I say.

"Yeah, OK."

A horn toots outside. We go get his stuff from the barn and he goes home.

Back in the house I get a sandwich. What in the world could make those weird patterns? Or was it something out of this world?

I don't really buy the idea of aliens. But something did it. We weren't both dreaming the same dream. I need to figure this thing out.

So I log onto our super slow dial-up internet and look up tree crop circles. Nothing. Just some crop circles that look like a tree. No circles made from trees.

So much for that. This is really going to drive me nuts.

◆ ◆ ◆

Next morning is church.

I always have a hard time paying attention, but some of the pastor's words break through to my brain as I sit here doodling on the bulletin. He's reading from the last part of the book of Job.

It's talking about all the awesome things God does and knows. Junk that he doesn't tell anyone, like where the gates to death are and stuff.

I guess he likes keeping secrets. He's sure been keeping them from me. No matter how often I ask him where my mom is...not a word.

After church I get on my bike and go downtown for an ice cream. I want to do some thinking about all that's happened in the past week.

As I'm riding by the park The Old Guy Who Lives in the Park calls me over.

"Match, could you get me a burger and fries?"

I told you he never leaves the park. He just has someone get stuff for him. The park people leave the tool shed unlocked for him. It's heated so he has a warm place to sleep when he needs it.

The Old Guy uses the tools to take care of the park, so the city started paying him for that. He doesn't have to beg or anything, other than to ask people to get stuff for him.

"Sure." I hold out my hand for the money.

"Get yourself a Coke, while you're at it," he says.

He always tips his delivery people.

I come back with his food and start to move on.

"Have a seat," he says. "I could use a little company." He puts aside a book he was reading.

Man, I have things to think about. I really don't want to talk, but I sit next to him on the bench and sip my Coke.

"You look distracted, buddy. Something on your mind?"

Oh, just weird circles of trees, vanishing

plants, and disappearing people. Especially disappearing moms.

I decide to go with the safest option.

"Did you know a guy named Stan?"

"Is he that nasty fellow?"

"Yep."

"I haven't had a conversation with him, but I've seen him around. He cussed me out a few times."

"What'd he cuss you out for?"

"Seems like he doesn't need a reason."

"Yeah," I said.

"Why are you bringing him up?"

"He's missing." My heart pounds just talking about it.

The Old Guy licks some ketchup off his wrist. "Is he now? Well, that's interesting."

I just nod and make that loud noise with my

straw that most adults hate. You know, trying to get the last drops of pop out of the ice.

"So it's a mystery, I guess," he says.

"Yeah. His dad is worried about him. He lives in the home and can't do anything about it, you know?"

"I see." He nods.

"I feel bad for him. He asked me to help, but…" I toss my cup into the trashcan. "I wouldn't know how, you know? Plus, like, everyone hates that guy. I don't think anybody would be much help."

"Well now. I guess that is a problem." He wads up his empty burger wrapper. "There is probably no point in trying."

I scuff my foot on the ground.

"Let the sheriff do it, it's her job, anyway. You just enjoy your summer." He looks at me over the top of the glasses that someone gave him.

Yeah, like the sheriff has done such a great job finding Mom.

"I don't know. I mean, maybe I could find something she missed. Maybe, since she's trying to find two people, she could use some help?"

"What could you do that she can't? I mean, she's a trained professional. You're just a kid."

I don't have to listen to this. I stand up.

"Whoa. Sit back down, buddy." He puts his hand on my arm.

I turn towards him, but don't sit. "Dude, I'm not a kid. And the sheriff hasn't done all that great a job so far. If people are going to get found it means someone's got to look. It might as well be me. Mr. Mac did ask and all."

He tosses his trash into the can and stands up. "I gotta get to work, but if you need anything, you know where to find me."

He grins at me and holds out his hand. Dude, I've been played. Oh well. I grin back and shake his hand.

8

The next day I ride my bike up to Stan's trailer. I can at least have a look around. That doesn't mean I'm going to play detective or anything. I'm just going to see if there's anything obvious.

He lives a mile out of town in the woods, but he always seems to be in town harassing people.

My hands and arms get tingly from the vibration of the gravel road. When I get onto his driveway, I have a hard time riding through all the crisscrossed ruts. The trees grow close to the drive and there are pinecones all over.

The only reason I even know where he lives is because Dad and me came up here to get a TV fixed one time. Stan fixes all kinds of stuff and it's best to have him do it at his place. Most people don't want him in their house. He makes messes, noses through stuff, and just acts creepy.

As I round the last bend of his long driveway, I hear ferocious barking. Shoot. I forgot about his evil dog.

I stop the bike and stand still a minute, ready to tear out if I have to.

The dog is in a small pen, jumping up against the fence. He's mad. I can tell. I don't know what kind he is but he's big. He's got a big old body like a Rott, and a small pointy head like a Doberman. He's definitely not a real kind of dog.

Stan's truck is here. Maybe he's just been hiding out for some reason. I look around and listen. All I hear is barking. The trees and dead brush are so thick someone could be watching me right now and I wouldn't see them.

Two dishes lay upside down near the dog. No water. No food. I guess Stan is gone.

Either that or...hurt? Dead?

Dude, Stan's been missing a week. I wonder how long the dog's been without food and water.

I put my bike down and pick up a long, thick stick and start poking at the dishes with it. If I can just...

The stick catches one of the dishes just right and I flip it over and pull it toward the fence. I fill the dish from the hose and the dog attacks the water. He'll probably make himself sick.

I try to get the other bowl the same way, but

can't. Darn it.

I don't have any food anyway. I look around again to see if it's out here somewhere.

There's an old rickety shed nearby. As I get closer I hear tap...tap...tap. Like somebody knocking weakly. I look around but no tree branches are touching the building. I was hoping maybe that's what caused the sound—tree branches.

My hands break into a sweat and I wipe them on my jeans.

Maybe Stan's in there.

Maybe he's been in there all this time. Hurt. Dying.

Maybe he's already dead.

Maybe his body is hanging in there banging against the wall.

Maybe what I hear is some wild animal

eating him.

Maybe I should just go home.

I turn around to leave, but, what if someone else is in there? What if he tied someone up and kept her in there and now she's knocking, hoping someone will help her?

What if it's...what if...?

Maybe he has Mom.

I turn back around. The door eases open. I peek through the crack. It's too dark.

The tapping is faster.

It's louder.

It's right beside me. My heart is just as fast and just as loud. I take a big breath and shove the door open.

A flutter and flurry erupt in my face and a bird whizzes past my head.

I lean against the doorframe and take a few

breaths.

Stupid woodpecker.

I let my eyes adjust to the dark. Weak stripes of light come through gaps in the walls. All I see are tools and lawnmowers and a bunch of other junk.

I don't know whether I'm relieved or disappointed.

Well, I came here to find clues, so I guess I need to try the house.

And I need to keep my imagination under control. I peer into the trees and bushes as I cross the pine needle covered dirt. The dog is still snarling at me.

There's no answer to my knock so I try the knob. It's unlocked. My heart starts thumping again. Is this illegal? Am I becoming a delinquent?

I push the door open and wait for a minute,

listening, then I say, "Hello?"

Again, a little louder, "hello?"

I step through the door, "Anyone here?"

Silence.

I sniff the air because I know that dead bodies stink, but it just smells like an empty house.

The place is clean and orderly. I guess I expected someone as rotten as Stan to live in a dump.

There's a big bag of dog food in the kitchen, so I grab it and pull it out the front door. Evil Dog starts whining when he sees me. I heft it up and dump a bunch over the fence.

He dives right in and his tail thumps against a tree like a drum.

Back inside the trailer I creep from room to room. I have no idea what I'm looking for. In Dad's cop shows there's usually a note in the trash, a check, some message from a phone call, or something.

I go to the phone. No answering machine. If he has voice mail, I have no idea how to check it.

I shuffle through some papers stacked on the counter, but nothing looks interesting. Bills mostly.

Wait…an appointment with Mrs. Johnson. Her dishwasher needed fixed. The date was last week. The last day that Mr. Mac said he spoke to Stan. Maybe this is a clue. I guess I could go talk to Mrs. Johnson. Just to see if there's anything obvious or anything.

I go to the door and turn the doorknob but hear a car pull up. I lock the door real quick and go peek out the window. It's the dogcatcher. Loretta is with him and they both get out. She comes up to the door and knocks. I hear the doorknob rattle.

"Nobody here," she says. "But I could have sworn the place was unlocked."

She rattles the knob again and then goes over to the dog pen.

"I can't believe you lost the order to come out here and get this dog," Loretta says.

"I know. I know. You nagged me enough in the truck. Let's just get this done." He opens the gate and sticks in a long pole with a leash on the end. "Looks like someone has been taking care of him, anyway. He's got plenty of water and food."

"Yeah." Loretta puts her hand on her gun and starts walking around, looking at the ground. Foot prints. Oh oh.

"I think someone has been here, but I can't tell for sure with all these pine needles."

Shoot. My bike. I look to where it's laying on the ground next to a bush. Maybe she won't see it.

"All righty, let's get this fella to the shelter." The dog guy shuts a little door on the truck.

"You won't adopt him out, or... anything, until we find out what happened to Stan, right?" She says.

"You bet."

They climb into the truck and drive away.

Dude.

9

I decide to go to Mrs. Johnson's house. I know where she lives because she and Mom were friends. It's kinda weird going alone.

When she answers the door I realize I don't know what I'm going to say.

"Match! What are you doing here?" Her long brown hair is wet, but she's got on makeup and a pretty dress. I've never seen her in anything else. My mom used to talk about it because she was — is—pretty much a jeans person. She felt like she ought to wear dresses sometimes, but she never did.

"Um, Hi."

"Hi." She looks around like maybe she expects someone else to be with me. "Do you want to come in?" She asks when I just stand there looking stupid.

"OK."

Inside she motions for me to have a seat.

Mrs. Johnson always had a box of toys for me to play with when Mom came to visit. They were cooler than the ones I had at home, so I loved coming over here. Plus she made the best sugar cookies. Also, she had these cups that were made out of, like, aluminum or some kind of metal and when you put an iced drink in them they got really cold and all dewy on the outside. I loved those cups.

I sit down, thinking about all these things, and my heart hurts because I can't be here and not think about Mom.

"I'm sorry that I don't come and see you sometimes, Match. I told myself that I would see how you were doing sometimes. Not to try to be your mother, but... you know. Just to check on you."

She picked at an afghan that hung over the side of her chair. "I guess good intentions don't count for much."

"That's OK, Mrs. Johnson. Dad and I are doin' all right."

"Yeah? I hope so. I know it can't be easy. But you've got a good dad."

"Yeah."

"So, Match, what brings you to my house? Hey," she stands up, "I just baked some cookies.

Do you want some? I know you used to love them."

I don't even have time to say "shoot, yeah" before she goes into the kitchen. The phone rings. She peeks through the door, her hand over the receiver.

"I'm sorry, this is important. I'll be a few minutes." She ducks back into the kitchen.

I hear her go outside, her muffled voice coming through the door.

I guess I shouldn't waste this opportunity, you know?

I get up and walk down the hall. There are three doors. The first one opens into a bedroom. It's all neat and unused looking. Probably a guest room. Not likely to be any clues in there.

I listen in the hall before moving on. She's still outside.

The next door is a bathroom.

The third door is her bedroom. It's pretty neat, but there are papers and books on the table by the bed. Probably if she had clues, they wouldn't be out in the open.

I listen a minute—she's still talking—then I look at the closet. Mom taught me it was wrong to nose through people's stuff. But there may have been a crime committed. Someone needed to do something, right?

The closet door slides open easily. Lots of clothes. Shoes on the floor. The top shelf only has a bunch of sweaters piled on it. Aren't people supposed to keep secrets in boxes up there?

A noise makes me jump. Her voice is louder. Oh my gosh.

I slip out the bedroom door and into the bathroom. I get the door closed just as I hear,

"Match? You still here?"

My voice cracks a little when I say, "Yes," then I flush the toilet.

I lean my head against the door a minute before I step into the hall. She's standing there looking at her open closet door. Then she turns and looks at me. She doesn't look happy. I duck my head and return to the living room.

A plate of cookies is on the coffee table along with one of those awesome cups with milk in it.

She comes into the room and sits across from me, still looking perturbed.

I pick up a cookie and take a bite but it kinda globs up in my mouth and is hard to swallow. She's watching me. She wants an explanation, I can tell. I hate that I've disappointed her.

"Um, see, it's like this," I say after taking a drink of cold, cold milk. "You know Stan?"

She narrows her eyes a little and nods.

"So, I'm kinda trying to figure out where he is. I mean, I know he was a jerk and all…."

"And you thought he'd be in my closet? I can't stand the man, why would he be here?"

"I know. I just… I heard that you saw him that day. I heard that he had an appointment here."

"And where did you hear that?"

Like I'm gonna tell her I was sneaking around his trailer.

"Um, I just heard it around and I thought that if he was here fixing something or whatever that he might have said something about what he was planning or something. I know he liked to talk and brag and all."

"He didn't say anything. And that doesn't explain the closet."

"Well, I..."

"Match, you're a good boy, I think. But you really overstepped your bounds today. I'd like you to leave."

I ain't gonna cry or nothin' but dang it. I stand up, cookie crumbs dripping from my shirt, and walk to the door. Before I step out I look over my shoulder. "I'm sorry Mrs. Johnson."

I'm walking down her sidewalk to my bike when someone says, "pssst." I look around and see an old lady is in the next yard motioning me over.

When I get to the fence she leans in close. "How is she doing today?"

"Uh, fine."

"Really? That's good."

"Why?"

"She's been... well... she's been having some

mood problems. Seems depressed and some days she throws all kinds of fits. I can hear her from my kitchen!"

"Really?"

"She told me she just discovered that she's allergic to chocolate. That could make anyone crazy, I guess."

"Do you remember when she had her dishwasher fixed a couple of weeks ago?"

"Oh my. When that nasty Stan came over?"

I nod.

"She really made a ruckus that day. I wouldn't be surprised if the whole neighborhood heard her hollering."

"What was she saying?"

"I couldn't make it out. But she was mad as a hornet about something, that's for sure."

"What time did Stan leave?"

"Well, you know, I'm not sure. I took a nap, like I always do. I suppose he left sometime while I was sleeping."

Dude. That does not sound good.

Now what? I mean what if she did do something to him? What can I do about it? I don't think I'll be back in her house any time soon. I'm sure she got rid of any evidence anyway.

Besides, I like Mrs. Johnson. Could she kill someone? Even if she is allergic to chocolate?

I say good-bye and turn to leave.

"Oh, by the way," she says, "you haven't seen a rhododendron anywhere have you? I can't find mine. It's like it vanished."

Oh great.

I shake my head and walk away.

10

From Mrs. Johnson's I go over to the sheriff's office because it can't hurt to see what she's found out. Loretta is my cousin. She's like fifteen years older than me so people always call her my aunt. I used to correct them, but they can't seem to grasp it any other way.

Her office has that weird old building smell. It's the original town hall, built over a hundred years ago when this town was a mining boomtown.

There are a few green metal desks scattered around and a jail cell at the back of the room.

Loretta is the only one here. Her deputies are usually out patrolling the county. She's sitting at her desk braiding her hair. It's really long. Dad calls her a granola girl.

"Hey there, Match. What's up?"

"I was wondering if you found out anything about Stan."

"Stan? Why are you interested in him?" She leans back in her swivel chair, and puts one of her feet on the table. She's wearing pink hiking boots. They look dumb with her sheriff uniform.

I sit in the chair across from her desk. "I just...." I shrug.

I know she'll say to mind my own business no matter what I say. She always bosses me around. Drives me nuts.

"Personally—although it isn't professional of me to say so—I think this town's better off with him gone." She raises an eyebrow.

I nod, because mostly I agree with her. But still. Mr. Mac deserves to know.

"There isn't anything to tell, anyway," she says.

I lean forward, my elbows on her desk. "Well, are you even looking?"

"We put the report into the database. But he's a grown person and grown people come and go all the time."

I take in a breath through my nose and lean back into my chair.

"Sorry, Match… I wasn't thinking." She gets up and pours a cup of coffee. "Anyway, the thing is, it's a free world…"

"Is not…" I interrupt.

"Free country—whatever. You know what I mean, and if Stan wants to leave town awhile, what's it to us?" She comes and stands by her desk, looking down at me.

"But.... Have you talked to Mrs. Johnson? I mean, she might know something."

"Mrs. Johnson? What are you talking about?"

I shrug.

She looks at me down her nose. "We did talk to her, actually, not that it's any of your business."

"And... did you find out anything?"

"Match... what would we find out? We just wanted to know if he mentioned going anywhere while he was at her house." She looks at me funny and then stares into the corner by the coffee pot for a minute.

She bends down and looks in my face. "Hey, you haven't been out to Stan's house by any chance have you?"

"Of course not," I say. My heart is thumping because I hate lying. I stand up.

"All right." She doesn't look convinced, but she slides into her chair. "You just mind your own business and keep out of this."

"But…"

"Again, I have to ask, why are you interested, Match? He's nothing but an old crank."

"His dad is my friend. That's why. He can't do anything to find him and someone has to. Sometimes even old cranks have someone who cares about them. People shouldn't just disappear without anyone caring." I feel my eyes start to sting so I turn around and walk out the door.

◆◆◆

When I get home the Roys are in front of the barn with some horses. Ray is already mounted up and Ron is tightening the pack behind his saddle. They get to use the horses on their days off. Dad calls it a perk.

Ray is wearing full on cowboy gear—chaps and everything, like he's going on a roundup. But he dresses like that now and then when he's not wearing his cape. I tell you, the guy is complicated.

Ron's just wearing jeans and a t-shirt.

"Hi, guys. What's up?" I ask.

"We're going up to look for Bigfoot. He's been sighted not far from here, you know.

Bigfoot. Dude. Just a few days ago I'd laugh at them.

"We're taking our cameras," Ron says.

"You wanna come with us?" Ray asks.

With the luck I've been having, I'd probably find him. And I don't think I can handle any more freakish paranormal experiences right now.

"Nah. Thanks, though. You guys have a good time!"

"We will!" And they take off. I'm relieved to see them going in a direction away from the tree circles. I can imagine the hullabaloo they would stir up if they found those things.

◆ ◆ ◆

I put in a DVD to watch an episode of Psych. Dad comes in and plops next to me. His stinky feet on the coffee table.

"Those kids are whippersnappers. They need someone to teach them a lesson. Smart alecks."

Dad doesn't really like Gus and Shawn. But it's my night to choose. Dad gets four nights a week when he watches his old movies and junk. He doesn't like me complaining about those, but he always feels free to complain about my choices.

After the crime is solved we go out to do some evening chores. It gets dark early here. The mountains that surround us give us a late sunrise and an early sunset. Some nights when there's no moon it is darker than the inside of a cow. We take our flashlights to the barn. The horses are snorting, stomping, and neighing. Something's up.

Wilma runs around in circles snarling and growling and yapping like she's got rabies. Dad and I both take off running. I open the barn door and flip on the light. Nothing. Just horses as far as I can tell. I look around for snakes, poking in the hay with a pitchfork.

Dad comes huffing in, holding his side and gasping for breath. He isn't much of a runner.

"What is it?" he says.

"Nothing. I can't find anything."

I go back outside and look around the barn and sniff the air. No smoke. I stand still and listen. The horses have quieted. I can't hear anything. I look around and see a weird glow in the hills in the same area where that circle is. Sorta greenish. Eerie.

I wonder if those Roy boys are up to something. Doing some kind of science experiment like building a particle accelerator or something. I hope it's not them. I don't want them anywhere near that circle.

I look for Dad, but he's in the barn. I hear him calming the horses. Maybe I should call him out here….

The weird light blinks out. Oh well. He'd probably just say it was a campfire or something.

I shudder and go into the barn. I've got to go up there tomorrow, see what's going on. Plus I want another look at that circle. Maybe I can figure out what it is.

We finish up our chores and go back to the house.

11

In the morning I get on the computer and look up "green glow." No luck. Just stuff about glowing fish and things in the ocean, and it's an understatement to say we aren't near an ocean.

I call Bean because he should go up there with me.

"There was a funky green glow on the mountain last night. I'm gonna go check it out. Can you come?"

"Green glow? What do you mean?"

"I don't know. Just that. It was there, then it wasn't. Near where that circle is."

"Far out! Yeah, I can go. I need to be back in time to help Mom clean the shop tonight, though."

"Cool. Get here as soon as you can."

After we saddle up, we take the same trail we used last week. The breeze is chilly. I'm glad I have my jacket on. You never know what the weather's going to be like, even in June. We've even had snow this late a few times.

"So, tell me about this glow," Bean says.

"The horses were acting all weird. Spooked, you know? So Dad and I were checking around to see what was up. Looking for prowlers or snakes or something. While I was looking around outside I saw this green glow up here. It was... I don't know. Just green and glowing. Then it just, like, turned off."

"Weird, man. What do you think it was?"

"No idea. I tried googling, but didn't find anything."

We tie up near the stream and let the horses graze while we walk the same direction we went before.

Wilma follows along, sniffing at the ground. Her hackles are up, but she isn't cowering like she did last time.

I can still smell that weird odor.

When we get to the top of the rise there it is, a big old circle of overlapped pine trees. I sit down and stare. How can this be real? My heart pounds. I thought it wouldn't be scary this time, but, dude, it still is.

Bean just stands there with his mouth open. Guess it still scares him, too.

I stand up and scan the area but don't see any

sign of green glowing stuff.

But wait, what's that? Just a few yards from the circle… another one. Whoa!

"Dude." I nudge Bean and point.

"Holy smoke," he says.

We move to a better vantage point. Wow. This is some wicked stuff. This circle is fancier than the other one. Instead of just one circle this one has a center circle with a bunch of little ones around the outside. Now my heart is pounding extra. What in the world is going on?

◆ ◆ ◆

Liz is at her desk when I go into the nursing home. She has green hair today, held back with a colorful scarf. She dresses weird all the time. She has to wear scrubs at work, but they are always goofy.

Like ones with ladybugs, or butterflies. Sometimes she wears ones with teddy bears like she works with kids or something. She says you have to find fun where you can.

When you see her out in the real world she's always dressed funky. Sometimes she looks like an old time Hollywood star or something. Other times she looks like a punk rocker. Everyone is used to it. We don't even notice, really. Except at church. She goes to my church and some of those people look at her pretty weird sometimes.

Liz and I used to have some weird conversations when my mom worked here. I decide to get her opinion.

My feet slip out from under me just as I reach the high desk around the nurses' station. I throw my arms over it to keep from falling and hang from it a minute like a kid does at the roller rink. I pull myself up, face hot. Maybe she didn't see.

She saw. Her lips are tight, trying not to smile, and she's shaking her head. I decide to just pretend it didn't happen.

"Liz," I say, "do you believe in weird phenomena?"

She looks up at me. "Like what?"

"Uh, like crop circles, junk like that?"

"Sure."

"Really?" I guess I should have figured. "But you're a Christian. Isn't that stuff weirdoes believe in?"

She gets up and walks around to where I am and leans against the wall.

"Matt, here's the thing. God is bigger than we can even begin to imagine. This stuff just means we don't have to understand everything."

"Yeah. I guess."

She winks at me and goes back to her paperwork.

She's probably right, but I kinda like understanding, though.

❖ ❖ ❖

Mr. Mac is in his room this time, digging through a box of papers and stuff. I stick my earplugs in.

"Hello," I say as I knock on the doorframe.

"Well, hi there, Little Mac. Come on in." He clears a spot on the chair next to his bed.

"Have you heard anything from Stan?" I sit on the stiff vinyl chair. Some folks have nice furniture from home or something, but Mr. Mac is stuck with the nursing home stuff.

"No, I haven't heard a thing." He looks out the window a minute.

"I've been trying to see if I can find out anything, but…"

"Why thank you. I appreciate that. I'm thinking that scoundrel just up and took off, though he never had much use for me apart from asking for money. I guess he wouldn't see the need to tell me goodbye or anything." He rubs his thumbs together while he talks.

"I guess. Maybe. That seems to be what everyone thinks. But…his truck is at his house. Does he have another car?"

Mr. Mac looks at me a minute. "Well…no, he doesn't. But maybe he left with someone else. That boy has friends all over the state, although I sure don't know why." He picks up a picture of a young boy. "You know, he used to be a good kid. It all went wrong after high school."

I look at the photo of a young Stan. "What

happened?"

"He and a friend were out carousing and they got in an accident. His friend died and Stan never forgave himself."

"Was he driving?"

"Nope, but he says he caused the accident. Won't say what he did, but still thinks it was his fault." He tosses the picture into the box. "He started getting ornery and just kept on getting worse."

Wow.

I watch Mr. Mac dig through some more papers.

He smiles and holds out an old black and white picture, crumpled at the corners. It's him, I guess, a lot younger, with a pretty woman. She is looking at him like he's a movie star while he grins at the camera. Makes me think of what Stan might look like if he didn't have so much meanness carved into his face.

Stan might have just took off, but seems like there are some people who took more than a dislike to him. Would any of them actually do something to him, though?

12

I'm riding my bike to the grocery store for a candy bar when Mrs. Holmes hollers. "Mark! Mark, come here."

I sigh and think about pretending I don't hear, but my mom really emphasized being polite. It's such a pain. Somehow I worry more about disappointing her now than I did when she was actually around to be disappointed.

I stop my bike and trudge up the walk.

"Hurry up, boy. You think this is the 26th

century or something?"

I pick up my pace just a little.

"Mark," she says when I arrive on her porch. She has foil pie pans hanging from the roof. Looks like they go all the way around her house. "More of my plants disappeared. *And* four other people in the area have had plants disappear as well. These will stop them from bothering me, though." She points to the disks glinting in the sun. "They interfere with the signals."

She looks down at me without tilting her head.

I don't know why she's telling me this, but I'm creeped out.

"Well..." I say.

"It's those horrible Boogonians." She leans forward, "But I'm getting the situation under control, Mark. So don't you worry."

She pats me on the arm and then goes into her house.

Maybe I should set up a plant stake out. But I'd never be able to guess which plants to watch.

◆ ◆ ◆

The Roys were supposed to be back yesterday, but when I go outside the horses haven't been let out and Missy and George—the horses they borrowed—are still gone. Dad and I do their chores, but we're worried because those guys take their job seriously and have never missed work before.

Yesterday afternoon Dad called the sheriff.

This morning when I finish my chores the Search and Rescue are here. They're unloading some horses from trailers. One of them unloads an

ATV. Dad and Loretta are talking to them so I head over there.

"You need anything, let us know. We will do whatever we can to help you find those boys," Dad says.

The guy in charge nods. "We appreciate that."

He looks over at me. "You the last to see 'em?"

"Yeah."

"Which way were they going?"

I point in the direction I last saw them.

"All right then. Thanks. We'll let you know what we find."

"Thanks," Dad says. His eyes look small and his mouth is pinched.

Then he says, "I think we should pray," and bows his head right there in the driveway and starts praying. He does things like this now and then. Embarrasses me, then I get embarrassed for being embarrassed.

After he finishes asking for God to help out the rescuers and Ron and Ray, the searchers take off.

Loretta says, "I will keep in touch with them by radio and let you know any news," then gets in her Jeep and leaves.

Dad goes into the house and I think about disappearing plants, green glows, and crop circles. I wonder if I should tell him about those tree circles. Could they have anything to do with the Roys going missing? But they went to a completely different area. And besides, I'm the one that made a big deal about not telling anyone. I can't go back on that now.

◆ ◆ ◆

In the night I wake up. Something doesn't feel right. I get up and go into the living room. The TV is on but Dad's not there. It's one o'clock; he's usually in bed by now.

I peek into his bedroom, but it's empty. Then I glance in the bathroom, but he's not there either. My heart speeds up and my hands are moist. I wipe them on my pjs and go into the kitchen. My voice echoes as I call for him. No answer. I turn on the tap and my hands shake as I take down a glass and fill it with water. The small sip catches in my throat and I walk back into the living room.

"Dad?" I hate the way my voice quivers. But where the heck is he?

I go to the window and pull the curtain aside. Just as I peek out I hear the front door open and Dad clomps in. I jump like a little kid, splashing water all over myself.

"Dad!"

He jumps a little, "What are you doing up?"

"I, uh, just needed some water. Where were you?" I hope he can't hear how tight my voice feels.

"The horses were riled up again so I was checking on them. Go back to bed." He clicks off the TV and goes to his room.

I look out the window again toward the barn. Then I look beyond up to the hills and see that weird green glow hovering just above the treetops. As I watch they stop and all is pitch black. Dude.

◆ ◆ ◆

The next morning when I come out from doing

chores in the barn, I see some riders coming out of the woods. Sure enough, it's Ron, Ray, and the searchers. I radio Dad, who's out on the back forty, then I take their horses and settle them in the barn.

When I come out, the Roy boys are sitting in the lawn chairs under a tree drinking some water.

"Where were they?" I ask one of the searchers.

"Oh, they weren't all that far. Just up that rise a ways. Still took us a long time to find them." He pushes his hat back and rubs his head. "Idjits were underground."

I look over at them sitting there rubbing their feet.

Ray glances at me, "Mine shaft."

"Yep," the searcher says. "They were digging around up there and weakened an old shaft, fell right down."

"What were you digging for? Bigfoot?" I say.

Ron shakes his head. "We thought we found some gold."

"So they wandered around down there in the mine awhile then ended up back under the hole they fell through." The Search and Rescue guy says. "Fortunately it wasn't very deep, so they didn't get hurt. There was a little spring so they had some water." He shakes his head. "Idjits."

"We didn't mean to fall in a hole," Ray says. He's covered in a fine coating of dust. "We already said we're sorry."

Ron shakes dirt out of his hair. "Yeah. We're sorry, already."

Dad drives up and hops out of his truck. The story is told all over again. Turns out the reason the searchers are so aggravated is because there was slag all over the place. To Ron and Roy the leftover rock from old mining operations meant that there could still be gold around. It should have made them realize the area would be full of mine shafts, too. Oh brother. At least they're OK.

"Any chance that Stan fell down one of them things, too?"

Everyone turns to stare at me. "I just, uh, I was just wondering, you know. I mean if it could happen to these guys it could happen to someone else, right?" Like maybe even Mom.

The searcher shrugs. "That guy that went missing last week?"

I nod.

"Nah. He wasn't much of an outdoorsman from what we understand. Of course anything is possible. We looked around up there but there weren't any signs that anything like that happened."

I shrug. Well. No way that Mom fell into a hole, either, I guess. She only went to the mountains when Dad or I was with her. She was afraid of bears.

13

I come out of my room in my pajamas. I'm not telling you what they look like, dude, they're just pajamas. After I fix a bowl of Cap'n Crunch I go to the living room to put in a Batman DVD. I always have to wake up slow, you know?

If Dad were still in the house he'd expect me to be dressed and getting started on my chores.

Voices come through the screen door from the porch. I peek out. It's Dad and Loretta sitting out there. I start to go back to my cereal when I hear Mom's name.

"Nothing new." Loretta says. "What is weird is that we haven't been able to trace anything. No credit cards. No plane tickets. No tickets for anything."

Dad grunts.

I've backed against the wall so they can't see me, but I can't see them either.

"There were no withdrawals from your bank…" She says.

"I know all this, Loretta. What I'm wanting is something new. Haven't you found anything at all?" I hear a chair scrape on the floor and foot steps. I look out. Dad's leaning against the porch railing, looking out at the view.

I didn't know any of that. I just thought nobody was trying very hard.

"I'm sorry, Fred. I'm just baffled. You didn't

have any cash around the house, did you?"

Mom did.

"If I did, don't you think I'd tell you?"

"Yeah. I guess so."

"I'm sorry, Loretta." I hear him pacing. "This just makes me so…. Consarn it. I just don't know who to be mad at. But I guess it ain't you. I know you're doing your best."

I step out the door. "Mom had a stash of cash."

They both look at me wide-eyed.

"What are you doing eavesdropping?" Dad says.

"Well, that's the only way I can find anything out around here."

"You don't need to be worrying about this."

"Dad, I'm not a baby. And, dude, I am worried about this. How can I not worry about this?" My hands are clenched up. "You treat me like I'm a little kid. Dude! You didn't even tell me she was missing. You told me she went to see her old college friend. Do you think I'm stupid? Did you think I wouldn't hear people talking about her? Did you think I wouldn't know they were talking about Mom when they talked about her running off, or being kidnapped? When they talked about where her dead body might be?"

He looks at his boots and Loretta looks at him.

I walk over to my bike and get on. "I'm not a baby," I say over my shoulder as I peddle away.

I'm already on the main road when I realize I still have on my pajamas.

◆ ◆ ◆

Bean and I sit at the Rocky Mountain Pie eating a Triple Dog Dare Ya pizza. It's got every kind of meat on it, and the only vegetables are jalapenos. He's drizzling honey on his and I'm sprinkling pepper flakes on mine.

We aren't talking much, just chowing down. I watch the people around us while Bean examines his pizza like it's a crime scene.

"Ron and Roy fell down a mine shaft." I say.

"A mine shaft? That's wild. How did that happen?"

"They were digging for gold."

"Oh. Makes sense."

Only to Bean. And the Roy boys.

"We should go up there and look at them circles again," he says. "Did you tell your dad about them?"

"No, Dude, I said we weren't supposed to tell

anyone. Have you told anyone?"

"Well, I just figured you might tell him, being the Roys went missing and all."

"Did you tell anyone? Have you told your mom?"

"Man, what do you think I am? I said I wouldn't tell anyone."

I stare at him.

"I haven't. I swear. Man."

I grab another piece of pizza and leave the pepper flakes off this time. My tongue is going numb as it is.

The waitress comes by and refills our root beer.

Bean finishes off a slice with honey on it and then gets up and walks toward the bathroom.

There's a couple of old guys sitting in the booth behind me. I don't know them, but I've seen them around. They're at the bottom of their second pitcher of beer so they're getting kinda loud and laughing a lot.

One says, "Guess they haven't had any luck finding that fella Stan." They have my attention now.

"Yeah. I bet they ain't tryin' all that hard. I wouldn't if I was them."

"Kinda like when that McGillicuddy woman went missin' a few months back."

Mom? I lean back further.

"Yep. 'Cept they looked long and hard for her, being related to the sheriff and all. The husband insisted she hadn't left him, even though we all know that's what happened. Women run out all the time. Probably got a hankering for some other fella."

My fists clench.

"Like Stan MacDonald."

Whoa. What did he say?

"Yeah. I bet he coulda' told someone where she was, but he was too ornery. He wouldn't help a baby out of a bull ring."

"Nope. He didn't help no one but himself. Still, seems like the ladies liked him well 'nough."

I'm like, practically leaning backward over the seat, but they change the subject to motor oil preferences and I slump forward and let out my breath.

I take out my wallet and unfold the piece of paper I keep tucked there.

Bean comes back and pours honey on another piece of pizza. I stick the paper back in my wallet before he sees it.

What did they mean hooking my mom and Stan together like that? I don't think she even knew the guy. But, they said he knew where Mom was?

Bean looks up from his trough. "Hey man, you OK?"

I nod.

"You look kinda sick."

I lean forward over the table.

"Those old guys behind me said Stan probably knows where my mom is."

Bean scrunches his face. "Why would he know that? That's bogus."

"Well, maybe. But it's something. If he knows where she is or if he did something to her…. Dude, I gotta find him now."

14

Bean and I are on Main Street, headed for the Milky Way for some ice cream when I see Emma coming out of the Rocky Mountain Pie. She's with this dude from school, Jerry. He's looking at her all fuzzy like.

I can't stand Jerry.

Emma giggles a little and then looks at me. She smiles all big and takes a step toward me, "Hi, Match" she says as she waves.

I wave as they walk past. And I stick my foot

out, just a little. Jerry trips and falls flat.

Emma bends over him to see if he's OK. She's touching his face and his arm.

Dude. I guess that backfired.

Jerry gets up, trying to act all cool. Emma looks like an attending angel or something.

Darn.

He turns and glares at me over his shoulder.

I sigh.

"Man, what's the deal?" Bean says, but he's smiling. I know he thinks I like Emma. He doesn't know anything.

"That's a total bummer, man, her being with that guy. He's so bogus."

"Doesn't matter to me," I say.

"Right," he says, but he's still got that stupid grin on his face.

Whatever. She can hang out with anyone she

wants. Besides, it's not like I can even talk normal when she's around. She's better off with someone with a brain.

I order some Rocky Road and Bean gets vanilla. He's got all those weird food concoctions but will only eat vanilla ice cream.

We sit at the table out on the sidewalk.

"So how are you going to find Stan, man?"

"I don't know, dude. I already looked around his trailer…"

"What? Did you go inside?" He nibbles the bottom off his cone.

I nod. "Nothing there, though. I talked to Mrs. Johnson because she saw him last as far as I know."

He raises his eyebrows.

"That didn't go well," I say. "I really don't know what else to do. It's not like I can check his credit cards or anything like that. Loretta won't tell me, like, anything."

"I guess we just keep asking around," he says.

"Yeah. People don't much like talking about Stan, though."

"I bet. Unless it's to gripe, right?"

I nod.

"I'll listen in at work. Those women are always gossiping and I usually have my iPod on, so I don't know what they talk about. I'll see if any of them know anything."

"Yeah. That's a good idea. Someone is bound to know like, something, you know? I guess I'll go talk to Loretta again. See if I can get her to cough up any info."

I lick the last drop of chocolate off my lip and then get up and wave. "I'll talk to you later."

"Later, man."

◆ ◆ ◆

Some guy comes barging out the door from the sheriff's office. Don't know who he is, but he looks mad, almost knocks me down. When I walk in, Loretta sticks her hand under her desk real quick. Probably a candy bar. We all know she eats them, but she acts like it's a crime. She's always telling people how she only eats raw honey, raw organic goat milk, and hemp seeds.

She glares at me. Great. She doesn't look very helpful.

"What do you want?" There's a brown smudge on her front tooth.

"I was wondering if you guys have found out anything about Stan."

She licks her teeth while she looks me over. "We already talked about this, Match. I can't tell police business to just anyone who comes in here asking."

This was a mistake. Whoever that guy was, he really set her off. I hate it when she gets like this. Because I'm her cousin, she feels free to take it out on me.

I put my hand in my pocket and rattle my change.

"I, uh... Well, did you look up his credit card and all that?"

She squints again. "I know how to do my job, bub. Don't come in here giving me the third degree."

"Sorry. I just can't believe he disappeared with no clues at all."

"I didn't say that. I said I can't tell you

anything."

She starts fidgeting and I figure the Snickers is calling to her.

"What is it you think I'm going to do with the info, Loretta? What could it hurt?"

She glances under her desk, "Again, I have to ask, why are you interested, Match?"

"You know, Loretta, you're supposed to be a public servant. Ser-vant. Got that? I'm the public. I'm here to be served. You don't want me telling you how to do your job, but I think someone needs to. It doesn't involve creamy caramel and chewy nougat."

She stands up, a mess of melted chocolate and goo globbed up in her hand.

"Go away, Match. You go do whatever it is you do and mind your own business."

◆ ◆ ◆

I decide to go to the nursing home. Mr. Mac is taking a nap. Liz is sitting at her desk with her blue hair all wadded up like she's been squeezing it or something.

"Hi, Liz. What are you doing?"

She looks up and sighs. "We finally got a computer. We're only twenty years behind." She grins at me. "Now I have to take all the information in these," she pats huge stack of files, "and put it in here." Her hair gets squeezed while she says it.

"Dude, that's going to take, like, forever."

She nods. "Hey, how about a cup of coffee? I could use a break."

I wrinkle my nose.

"Soda?" she asks.

"Sure."

We walk to the employee break room. "Do you need me to hold your hand?" she says. "So you don't fall?"

"Very funny."

We arrive safely. She gets a Coke out of the vending machine for me and pours herself a cup of coffee.

The coffee smell tingles in my nose. Dad doesn't drink it. Mom did. I close my eyes and picture her sitting there holding the cup instead of Liz. We used to do this on Mom's breaks when she worked here.

"You all right, Matt?"

I open my eyes and nod. "Just, you know, resting."

"You visit Mr. Mac today?"

"Nah, he's sleeping. I'll come back

tomorrow." I take a swig of Coke. "You know whether he's heard from his son?"

"Stan?" she wrinkles her forehead. "I don't know. He hears from him every week doesn't he?"

So, she doesn't know.

"Yeah, but not lately. He's worried about him."

"That jerk. Probably ran off. That's what he does." She stirs her coffee so hard some sloshes out onto the table.

"You know him?"

She looks at me a minute, her mouth real tight. "Yeah. I know him. That no-good…poop… used to be married to my sister."

"Really? I didn't know he was married."

"This was awhile back. Right after high school. I never liked the guy, but Sue was crazy about him. He didn't treat her like she deserved. I don't think he was terrible to her, but he sure could have been better…."

"Like what?" I ask.

"Well, he didn't want her to go out with her friends. Put her down a lot, you know, trying to make himself look better. Teased her in a mean way, that kind of thing. She didn't seem to care, though. She never had a bad thing to say about him."

She shakes her head and takes a sip of coffee. Then she just sits there looking into her cup. I'm not one for romance stories, but this story may be a clue.

"Well? What happened?"

"He ran off. Just took off one day and broke her heart. She fell apart. She hasn't been right since. I wonder if maybe something wasn't right all along." She looks off behind me, her eyes glazed and sad. "We had to have her put into a special home. She can't function on her own anymore."

"You mean she's crazy?"

She nods. "That jerk had the nerve to come back here and bring another woman. He walked around all over town with her and Sue couldn't take it. She... she got violent. Tried to hurt the woman." She takes another sip of coffee. "If Stan doesn't ever come back, it will be too soon for me." She looks vicious.

Wow. Even Liz hates the guy. And for good reason I guess. Does she hate him enough to do something to him?

I look at her over the rim of my Coke can. Her face is red and her eyes are cold. Could she do something like that? How well do we really know people anyway?

◆ ◆ ◆

When I come out of the nursing home, Bean is walking toward me. "I haven't heard anything at the shop," he says, "but Mom's going to keep her ears peeled. She loves detective books."

"Ears open, Bean. Eyes peeled, ears open."

"Eyes peeled? That's gross."

Mrs. Holmes hollers over the fence, "Boys! Can you come here a minute?"

We look at each other and shrug. It's always a bit exciting and a bit frightening to see what she's up to. Hopefully, she's been baking cookies.

We walk up the bumpy walk to her porch. She thrusts that creepy monkey into my hands. "Hold Mr. Nutsy. I have to go down to the basement and check on Steve." She rushes into her house.

I give the monkey to Bean who smiles and pets him. "Who is Steve?" I ask him.

He shrugs. "Probably one of her plants."

Bean plays with dumb Mr. Nutsy and I go to the other side of the porch. That thing wants to eat me. I know it. I can see it in his eyes.

Mrs. Holmes comes back out. "He's all right. Not going anywhere."

We both nod, but of course we have no idea what she's talking about. She hands us each a snicker-doodle and then tells us to go home. Bean gives the monkey back and we both stand there looking toward the door because we can smell cinnamon. Mrs. Holmes shoves the monkey back in my hands and goes inside. I throw the monkey on Bean and then we wait eagerly. She comes back with two cinnamon rolls wrapped in napkins.

"Don't tell anyone where these came from," she says. Then grabs the monkey and goes back inside. What a kook.

I wonder if Loretta knows how crazy this lady is. Does it matter? Is it illegal to be crazy? Maybe she should be in one of those special homes like Liz's sister.

This gets me thinking about Liz again. She could do it. You know, like with drugs or something since she's a nurse. She could kill a person if she were mad enough, maybe. But... really? I mean, she's one of the nicest people I know. But, if not her, who?

15

Bean and I wander down the street. Emma and her friend Ann come out of one of the boo-tee-cues. That's what my dad calls boutiques. Ann comes over and Emma stands back looking into a shopping bag with her face all red.

"Soooo, Matchie…" Ann says, standing on her tiptoes to get in my face. "I hear you like Emma." She wriggles her eyebrows at me. My face burns. There is only one person who knows how I feel about Emma. I turn and glare at Bean. He ducks his head.

I can't believe it. All our lives we've been friends and he's never told a secret before. Why this one? I look at Emma out of the corner of my eye. She's still digging in her shopping bag and her face is pink. Dude. I am going to kill him. I mean it.

"Match and Emma sitting in a..." Ann starts. She's so tiny. People might think she's a little kid if she doesn't stop acting like one.

"I don't know what you're talking about." I say and turn and walk away. When I get around the corner I peek around and see Bean standing there twisting his toe into the sidewalk, talking to Ann. Aha. I get it. You think you know a guy and then along comes a girl... Dude, she can have him.

I walk home faster than I ever have before.

◆ ◆ ◆

I'm riding my bike to see Loretta. I know she'll probably blow me off again, but I've worn her down in the past with my pestering. Who knows? I might, like, hit the jackpot this time. That is if she even knows anything. Sure doesn't seem like she's trying very hard.

I'm thinking if Stan went somewhere with someone, wouldn't he at least call his dad? I can't figure how leaving town would keep him from calling when he does it every week. I wish the police were doing more about it. They ought to be out looking for a body, or something.

The door to the sheriff's office is unlocked, but she isn't there. Nobody is. Usually they lock it when they're all out.

After looking around to be sure I'm really

alone, I move over to Loretta's desk and pull open the bottom drawer—the one that's like a file cabinet. The floor creaks and I jump. The room's still empty. Stupid old building.

Yep, there's a bunch of folders in here. I flip through the tabs and... wait. One has Stan's name on it. I look around again and pull the file.

The file is full of reports by different people accusing Stan of stuff. Right away I see Dad's name. It's on a report about when Dad's truck was "assaulted," as he puts it. Dude. This says he accused Stan. Loretta told him she couldn't do anything without any proof and it says that Dad "stormed out in a rage."

Wow. Dad's got a temper and all, but I've never seen him in a rage. I know he's overprotective of that truck. Could he really be mad enough to do something about it? Could he have hurt Stan? Dad always said he would kill anyone who messed with his truck, but he was just kidding. Right?

He's been extra irritable since Mom's been gone. Maybe this truck thing put him over the edge.

I put the report back and flip through some more but I hear the front door squeak open and voices in the small entryway. I shut the drawer and scurry to a chair across the room and drum on the wall with a pencil, trying to look bored.

"Can't you just let this drop?" I hear Loretta say.

"No, we can't. Once an accusation has been made we have to follow through on the investigation, Loretta. You know that." I don't recognize the man's voice.

"But he's nowhere to be found. How can it

matter now?"

"He made some serious allegations. We can't ignore felony menacing. Now you and I both know that you are not the kind of person to do the things that he claimed, but the law is the law."

"If the press gets ahold of this, I could lose my job, even if we don't find him." Her voice is tight, like she wants to shout, but is holding it back. "And if we do find him, it's just his word against mine. I could go to prison!"

Dude. Prison? I wonder what felony menacing is.

"We're going to do everything we can to see that doesn't happen. We all know what Stan is like. We know that his word has little value. Just hold tight, Loretta. You do what you can to find him, because when it comes out that he's lied about you, he'll have some charges to deal with himself."

"I don't care about that. I don't care if I never see the man again." She comes busting through the door that connects to the entryway and screeches to a halt when she sees me.

"What the heck are you doing here, Matthew?" She only calls me that when she's mad.

"Nothing," I say and scurry past her out the door.

I look up and down the street, trying to see who was talking to Loretta. A man in a dark suit with blond hair rounds the corner. I hop on my bike and go the same direction. I pass him and try to get a look without being obvious but can't really see much except the suit and blond hair. Not many people around here wear suits.

I go around the corner and turn around. Nonchalantly I pass him again from head on.

Yeah, I guess I've seen him around. But I don't know who he is. He's talking on his phone and gives me a slight nod.

Well, I'll keep my eye out for him.

What were they talking about anyway? Felony Menacing? I'll have to look that up.

Dang. What's with that Stan? What does he have against Loretta?

I stop in front of the sheriff's office and stare at the door. A person would do a lot of things to avoid prison.

Man, I'm getting nowhere with this thing. Seems like everyone in town has some kind of reason to want Stan gone. Even my own cousin. And my dad. Dude, I gotta figure this out.

Bean might know something. But I'm not asking that rat for anything again. Times like this I wish I had more than one friend.

I hear voices and see Bean, Ann, and Emma walking out of the candy store across the street. Bean sees me and waves me over. Dude. I don't think so. The fink. I got chores to do anyway.

◆ ◆ ◆

"Dad," I say as I dry the dishes, "is Loretta in trouble?"

He looks at me. "Maybe a bit. Why do you ask?"

"I just heard something and wondered what's going on."

"Nothin' for you to worry about it, Son. She's a tough 'un. She'll be all right."

"But... what's going on."

He scrubs at the chili pot. "Never mind. We don't need to be talkin' about it. It ain't nothin' anyway."

I can tell by the way his jaw's jutting out that he's not going to tell me anything. Darn it. He treats me like I'm still ten or something.

Mom would tell me. She told me everything. After I dry the pot I toss the towel on the counter and go to my room.

Who else would know anything? Loretta is kinda private, keeps to herself. I know she's got some friends but I don't know any of them.

Maybe I should figure out who that guy is.

I boot up the computer and type our county into Google. It comes up and I see a listing of all the government people with photos. There he is. The DA. That sounds like a big deal.

I put Felony Menacing into Google and get a result for Colorado. Basically it just means she scared him with a deadly weapon.

I laugh. I can actually see Loretta doing that. But leave it to Stan to make a big deal out of it.

I wonder if she really did it? Seems like a silly thing to go to prison over. I think she has more sense than that. Maybe.

I look at Dad, thinking of how mad he was about his truck. Being upset about Mom and then his truck just might have pushed him to violence.

I shake my head. I don't even want to think about that.

Then there's Mrs. Johnson and her strange behavior. She was the last to see him.

And Liz….

I sigh and turn on the TV and slide the Psych DVD in. Maybe Shawn and Gus have the answers.

16

Next day, just as I'm about to eat lunch there's a knock on the door. It's Bean. I look at him through the glass for a minute and he just stands there grinning at me. I open the door and walk over to the couch.

"Hey, man. How's it going?" he says.

I shrug. "All right."

"So, you wanna go on a ride tomorrow? I've been thinking I'd like to see that groovy circle thing again." He grabs a handful of chips out of the bag. "Got anything else to eat?" He eyes my sandwich.

"Dude. Eat before you come."

"What's your problem?"

"What's *your* problem? What's with you and your big mouth?"

"I'm just hungry, man."

"I mean blabbing to Emma and Ann."

"What?"

"You told them that I like Emma." I stand up, my fists tight.

"It's no big deal, man."

I shove him. "Don't tell me what's a big deal."

He shoves me back.

"I used to be able to trust you." I bang him into the table.

He puts his head down and runs at me like a

goat. Now I'm rammed against a wall with his head in my chest.

"Don't be such a wuss," he says, standing up. "She likes you too. I did you a favor, man"

Bam. I punch him right in the gut. Hard.

He doubles over and sits on the floor. Who's the wuss now?

After he catches his breath he says, "Geez, man. I didn't know it was such a big deal. Sorry."

I put out my hand and help him stand up. "Don't do it again."

"All right."

"You want mustard on your sandwich or honey?"

"Both."

◆ ◆ ◆

So we're riding up to see those circles again.

"Your mom say anything about Loretta?" I ask.

"Yeah. I think she's in some kind of trouble."

I rein in my horse. "Really? Do you know why?"

"Something about a gun."

Well, I guess that verifies my research.

"Heard anything about Stan?" I ask.

"People are talking about what might have happened. They seem to all think that he just took off. Probably with some floozy."

What? Like my mom? She is *not* a floozy.

My horse stretches her neck to get some grass and I pull her back and tap her with my heels to move on again. "Loretta's, like, got to go to court or something. She was talking to the DA."

"The DA?" Bean grabs at some overhanging

leaves. "Wow. She must have done something serious."

"Stan accused her of something. That doesn't mean she did it. You know he's full of it. But still, that DA guy says they have to investigate and all that."

"Man. That don't sound good."

"I guess she, like, scared him with her gun or something. I'd like to know the details, though, you know?"

"I'll ask at the shop and see what I can find out."

"Cool."

We take the horses off the trail toward the circle things. Wilma follows along, not even reacting this time. The weird smell is gone. That's probably what bothered her before.

The crop circles are still there. Of course.

Because, like, where would they go? But I kinda thought that maybe the forest guys might have found them and roped them off or something. I guess that would have been in the news, though.

We tie up the horses and wander around kinda hoping to see more, but if there are any, we can't find them.

"Dude, do you think aliens did this?" I say. "I mean, really?"

Bean just shrugs.

"What if they did? What if Stan was abducted?" My heart patters. "What if... what if they've been here before? What if Mom..."

"Man. Your mom wasn't abducted by aliens."

"How do you know?"

"Because... because, man, moms don't get abducted by aliens, that's how."

I look at him and shake my head. "Brilliant,

dude."

"Well... have you ever known any other mom who got abducted? Why would yours be the first?"

I guess he kinda makes sense. But still. As I look at these freaky bent trees, I can't feel too certain about it. I don't feel certain about anything.

◆◆◆

I'm in the barn cleaning the stalls. Dad says if they aren't done when he gets back from the store, I won't get my allowance. I was supposed to do it yesterday and he's kinda ticked, you know?

The phone rings in the house so I drop my shovel and run in to answer it. Probably someone selling something, but it's an excuse to stop shoveling manure, even if only for a minute.

"Hello?"

It's Bean. "You been runnin'?"

"What's up?"

"We gotta meet. I found some stuff out but I don't wanna' talk over the phone. How about lunch at Micky D's?"

"Sure. See ya then."

Dude. I wonder what he knows. I look at the clock. 10:30. I guess that's not too early to head out. So what if it's only a ten-minute ride? I'll pedal slow. I'll finish shoveling later.

◆ ◆ ◆

Bean's at the counter ordering when I come in. I get behind him and order a Quarter Pounder and fries. Bean carries away a tray with a fish sandwich, chicken nuggets and a cheeseburger on it. Then the guy at the counter hollers and holds up an apple pie that Bean forgot. I shake my head and go fill up my cup with Coke. Bean is making a suicide, of course.

We sit in a corner booth by the play area. The noise from the kids should drown out our conversation, Bean says. This must be real top-secret stuff. But then, this is Bean. He likes making a big deal.

He unwraps his fish sandwich and opens a container of BBQ sauce and then proceeds to pour the sauce on his fish. I notice that there's like, extra tarter sauce on there, too. I don't know how I can keep an appetite around this guy.

With a mouthful of food he says, "So... I heard something at the shop this morning." He dunks a french fry in his drink and shoves it into his mouth.

I watch him mangle more of his food for a minute. "Okay, dude? What?"

"You gotta listen to this, man." He slurps real loud on his drink and then burps.

"This lady starts talking about Loretta." He crams a bite of chicken nugget in.

"Yeah?"

"She's telling everyone this story. I guess this lady saw what happened." I can barely understand him, but I don't want to wait until he's finished eating. "She says that she's hoping she'll get to testify. She's a big fan of courtroom TV."

I look around to see if anyone is listening, but it's just a bunch of kids hollering and moms telling them to eat one more bite and stuff like that.

"So, dude, what happened?"

"Loretta pulled her gun on Stan."

"Wow. Why? What was he doing?"

"Nothin. This lady said that Stan went through a stop sign and Loretta pulled him over. They were talking through the car window and Stan was being a jerk—like usual. The lady could hear them because they were right in front of her house and she was by the window. She said Loretta made Stan get out of the car and he started calling her terrible names and saying all kinds of stuff about her not being a real cop. She said something like, 'I'll show you real cop' and she pulled her gun and told him to get down on the ground spread eagle."

I know I probably shouldn't be smiling, but, dude! That's like a real cop show or something. And also, who wouldn't be on Loretta's side? Who wouldn't like to have seen that?

But this means Stan had a real complaint against Loretta. How far would she go to protect her job?

"Did she arrest him?" I ask.

"No, the lady said that Loretta started looking around and then holstered her gun and told Stan to consider it a warning and to get going.

"Then after Stan drove off she said it looked like Loretta was crying."

We both look down at our trays. Mine has some empty wrappers on it. Bean's has smears of sauce, ketchup, mustard, and crumbs of all sorts all over it.

What a mess.

17

Liz stops me in the hall on my way to Mr. Mac's room. "Match!"

I stop and turn around in one motion but I should have known that was too tricky a move for these floors. I land right on my butt. I grab the rail along the wall and pull myself up.

Liz comes over and puts her hand on my arm. She's not laughing. She's not even trying not to laugh.

"What's wrong?" I say.

"Mr. Mac is sick."

"Sick how? Is he OK?"

"He has pneumonia."

I look toward his room. "Can I see him?"

"Yes. He's on antibiotics, so he's not contagious, but I want to warn you… he's pretty bad." She has that look in her eye people get when they worry about a kid, you know. All concerned, like she thinks I might break down crying right there.

I'm not going to cry, but that look on her face is enough to make my stomach feel funny.

I rush down to his room and peer in the door. There's a smell of menthol and other stuff I can't define. Sick smells.

I creep in and stand beside his bed. He's sleeping. I don't think I should wake him so I sit in the chair by his bed. His eyeballs move beneath the lids and his lips make a puffing with each breath.

He really doesn't look good. Kinda gray. There's an oxygen tube under his nose. Dude. What if he dies? What if I don't find out what happened to Stan in time?

Mr. Mac's eyelids flutter and he opens his eyes. "Hey there, Little Mac." He's not yelling. In fact, I can barely hear him.

"Hi, Mr. Mac."

"How are the girls treating you?" He bonks me on the arm with a knuckle.

"They leave me alone, Mr. Mac."

He grins but his face looks blurry and my eyes sting.

"I'm gonna find Stan. You get better, OK? Feel better and I'm gonna find Stan."

He pats my hand and nods. "I'm a tough old

goat. I'll be all right." He sputters a cough and closes his eyes again.

I jump up and get out of there as fast as I can. Stupid tears try to leak out. He may be old, but he's one of my best friends.

As I hop on my bike to go home I hear Mrs. Holmes, "Mark! Oh Mark…" I just pedal harder and pretend I don't hear her. I know it's rude. My mom would be ashamed, but I just can't deal with her craziness right now. Who knows what she wants? Talk to her trees? Massage the sidewalk?

I stop at the park and lean my bike against a tree and look around for The Old Guy Who Lives in the Park. I don't see him on the bench. He might be doing some work or something.

The grass has been recently mowed. The sweet smell tickles my nose. I go over to the shed where the tools and stuff are and look inside.

Nobody there. As I turn around there's a guy walking his dog. "Hey," I say, "Have you seen The Old Guy?"

The dog looks at me and wags his tail before exploring the sidewalk with his nose.

"They took him away. The sheriff. Put him in the back of their car and drove off."

What? The Old Guy? What could they want with him?

"Are you sure it was him?"

"Yep. No doubt about it."

"Well...why? Do you know why?"

"Nope. They were shoving him in there when I arrived and then they drove off with their lights flashing and everything."

Wow. I turn and walk toward my bike. "Oh, thanks." I say over my shoulder and the guy with the dog nods. The dog acts like his nose is glued to the ground as his master tugs on the leash to move on.

◆ ◆ ◆

I drop my bike on the sidewalk and run up the steps to Loretta's office. What is with her these days? Pulling guns on people—although, it was Stan, I'm sure a lot of people wouldn't blame her — and arresting old homeless guys?

She looks up at me when I come in. Her eyes big, but also a definite grumpy look to them. "What the...? Slow down, Match. What are you doing?"

"Where's the Old Guy? What did you do to him?" I look toward the holding cell, but it's empty.

"Here, sit down, Match. Relax." She points to

a chair.

I just stand there looking at her.

"We took him to the hospital. He collapsed while mowing the lawn."

I sit down. First Mr. Mac, now the Old Guy?

"He's going to be all right. But he's got to stay at the hospital awhile. They think it might be his heart. It might just be that living out there has taken its toll. We're trying to figure out what to do with him. It's really not a good idea to let him keep living out there. I'm trying to figure out how we can help him."

"Oh...He won't like living anywhere else."

"That's for sure. We tried awful hard to get him to live somewhere when he first came. But now it looks like we've got to find a way to get him an indoors home."

"Maybe he could live with us."

Loretta grins. "That's nice, Match. But I don't think your dad would be thrilled with that idea."

"Yeah. I guess not." Dad's never been real social.

She leans over her desk toward me. "We'll think of something. It's good of you to be concerned. I'll let you know when he gets out of the hospital, OK?"

"Thanks."

"We'll miss him at the Fourth picnic tomorrow." She chuckles. "He always acts like he's the host. Although I guess in a way, he kinda has been. The park is his home."

"Yeah. It will be weird with him gone."

I sit staring at her a minute while she thumbs through some papers on her desk.

"Um. Loretta, are you going to lose your job?"

Her eyebrows come together. "Why do you ask?"

"Dude, I heard you tried to shoot Stan." All right, so I'm exaggerating.

"Shoot Stan? Why would I do that? Listen, you've got the story all wrong."

"So what's the right story, then?"

She looks at her hands on the desk. "I might as well tell you. It's going to be in the paper anyway. I lost my temper. I did something really stupid. I pulled my gun on him. But I had no intention of shooting him."

She looks at me. I can tell she cares what I think of her. I'm glad. Sometimes I wish she were just a regular cousin, instead of being a cop cousin.

I smile. "I know. That's what I heard. I was just messin' with you."

She stands up and smacks the top of my

head.

"Brutality!"

"I'll show you brutality." She smacks me again and we both grin.

"So... you haven't seen him since?" I say, "I mean, I heard that he got you in a lot of trouble."

She leans back and squints at me. "What are you trying to get at? And no, he didn't get me into a lot of trouble. I did that myself."

I nod and stand up. "Thanks for telling me about The Old Guy."

"Welcome. Now let me get my work done."

I turn as I'm leaving and see her pull a Snickers out of her desk drawer.

18

Dad and I load up the truck with lawn chairs and coolers and blankets. We're going to the park for the day-long shindig, as Dad would call it, to celebrate the Fourth of July. Everyone in town spends the day in the park eating and running races and all that old fashioned stuff.

They have carts of food set up. You know like corn dogs and Navajo tacos and smoked turkey legs. We always take coolers of food, but I just eat junk from the vendors. Dad can have his bologna sandwiches.

I'm going to use this time, while everyone is pretty much in one place, to get as much info and clues as I can about Stan.

We drop our stuff under a tree and I head off looking for Bean. I find him at the hotdog stand. He's putting pineapple on his hotdog. It's already got onions, sauerkraut, and relish on it.

"Where'd you get the pineapple?" I look at the array of condiments.

"Brought it from home," he says, holding the can up for me to see.

I shrug and look around hoping for a glimpse of Emma. There she is over by the pond feeding ducks. We call it a pond. Some people might call it a large puddle. But it's big enough to attract a few ducks.

She's wearing shorts and a purple shirt.

Purple looks pretty on her. Anything looks pretty on her.

She turns her head and looks my way so I turn back around real quick.

Mrs. Johnson's right there. I almost run into her.

I look at my feet.

"Match," she says. "Listen. I've been pretty edgy and I feel bad about being so...forceful the other day."

Man. She really shouldn't apologize when I was the one rummaging through her things.

"It's OK. I mean, I'm sorry, too. I shouldn't have been snooping."

"Have you found any clues about Stan?" She says.

"No. Not really. Just lots of people who might be glad to have him gone."

She nods. "I bet. He left my house that day after he fixed my dishwasher. He got in his truck and drove away. That's all I know, Match." She smiles at me. "Come over for some cookies sometime, OK?"

"Okay, Mrs. Johnson."

She walks away.

Bean is finishing off his last bite of hotdog. "What was that about?"

"Ah, nothin'" I'm too embarrassed to go into it. "Dude, let's get some onion rings."

"All right." Bean follows me across the park toward the stand on the far side from the pond.

Loretta is there, pouring ketchup on her order.

"Match. Glad to see you. Mrs. Holmes called me this morning and asked me to bring her a hotdog and some onion rings."

"She called the sheriff's office?"

She nods.

"To order lunch?"

Loretta rolls her eyes and shrugs. "Would you take them over there for me?"

"Dude. Why me?"

"Because you do stuff for her. She's used to you. And because I know you're a good boy."

Now I roll my eyes.

"Hi Match."

I jump and turn around a little. It's Emma.

I can feel my face heat up. "Hi."

"What's up?" she asks.

Bean grins at me.

"Uh. Just, um, going to take some lunch over to Mrs. Holmes for Loretta." Like it was my idea all along.

Emma smiles. "I like Mrs. Holmes. Can I go

with you?"

Awesome, but, dude...no! What would I talk about? I look at Bean and he just grins. I look at Loretta and she hands me an order of onion rings.

"Go get her a hotdog with the works." She shoves a five into my hands. "She will pay you back, so bring me my money when you're done."

I look at Bean again and he turns and wanders off. Emma smiles at me. So I turn around and walk over to the hotdog stand. She follows.

"What have you been doing this summer?" she asks.

"Oh, the usual." Right. Like anything has been usual this summer.

She just nods.

"Actually, I'm trying to help a friend. You know Stan? He's disappeared and his dad really wants to know what happened to him."

"Wow. Like a mystery." She looks at me like I'm a hero.

I stand up taller.

"Yeah, well, pretty much. I mean, I guess it is a mystery." Along with missing moms and plants and creepy tree circles. I don't mention those.

I order the hotdog and then we walk south to Mrs. Holmes' house.

I can hear my heartbeat in my head. Why is this so hard? Last year I talked to her all the time.

"Mrs. Holmes asked me to mop her sidewalk the other day."

"Did you do it?" I ask.

She shrugs, "Yeah, why not? I mean, it was stupid and I felt dumb, but really, have you ever tried to *not* do something she asks you to do?"

I chuckle a little. "Yeah. That doesn't go over well at all."

Emma opens the gate since my hands are full.

Mrs. Holmes is sitting on her porch. "Mark, I hope you have my food. I've been waiting for hours." She grabs the food. "Hello Edna. I'm glad you came along, sweetie."

Emma smiles at her.

"Oh listen, Edna, since you're here, I really could use some help with Nutsy. He needs a bath. I used to do his baths, but lately, I just can't manage it. Could you come in and bathe him for me?"

Emma looks at me, eyes wide.

"It will only take about ten minutes." Mrs. Holmes grabs her by the elbow and ushers her through the door. "We don't need you, Mark. You go find something to do." And she closes the door.

I stand there on the porch wondering what I should do. I feel like I should have rescued Emma somehow. But how? Now that she's stuck I'll go over and see how Mr. Mac is doing and then I'll come and see if she's finished with the monkey bath.

Liz isn't here today. She's probably at the park. I go to Mr. Mac's room, hanging on to the rail to be safe.

He's in bed and looks even worse than last time. Wheezy noises are coming from his lungs and he has an IV going into his arm.

My chest hurts. He's just some old man. I mean, it's not like he's family or anything.

Dang it. He can't die. Maybe if I find Stan it will help Mr. Mac get well.

I whisper goodbye and go back to Mrs. Holmes' house.

Nobody is on the porch, so I ring the bell. No answer. I ring it again and knock. No answer. I pound harder. No answer.

The door is locked so I try to peek in the window but curtains are in the way.

Maybe the monkey bath is over and Emma is back at the park.

There are races being run when I get back. Sack races, that kind of thing. I look through the crowds but don't see Emma. I spot Bean holding a kid's hat just out of his reach. The kid is laughing and jumping for it. I wander over and Bean drops the hat. The kid grabs it and runs off.

"Hey, have you seen Emma?" I say.

"No, man, I thought she was with you."

"She was for a while. She was helping Mrs. Holmes and now I can't find her."

"She's probably around here somewhere."

"Yeah, I guess."

As much as I want to, I can't stop thinking

about Emma. I'm kinda hoping she'll sit with me tonight for fireworks. I'll just keep an eye out for her.

Bean and I watch some gunny sack races and relays. Last year we participated, but I can tell that Bean would be embarrassed to do it this year. We haven't even discussed it. Besides, it's pretty silly, you know? Trying to hop to the finish line in a bag, or run with your leg tied to another guy, or race with an egg in a spoon. We must have been dorks.

Someone taps me on the shoulder and I turn to see Emma's friend Ann. "Have you seen Emma? I thought she was with you."

"I thought she was with you." I look around. "I mean, she went with me to Mrs. Holmes' but I haven't seen her since she went in to wash the monkey."

"Wash the monkey? Oh brother. Do you think she's still there?"

"I knocked and rang the bell and there was no answer. I guess we could go try again. You sure she isn't here somewhere?"

"If she was, she would have found me. We were going to do the three-legged race together," She says.

I look at my phone to check the time. It's been about an hour since I came back to the park.

"Have you tried texting her?" I ask Ann.

We don't text much in these parts because the reception is so bad. But now and then you can get some bars and hope that the receiver has some, too.

"Yeah, but it didn't go through."

Where could she be? "Well, let's go back and see if someone will answer the door."

19

The porch is empty again. The front door closed. I pound on the door and ring the bell. Quiet. Nothing. I pound again. The door flies open and Bean, Ann, and I all jump backwards.

"What do you want, Mark?" Mrs. Holmes says. "Are you trying to raise the dead? Were you raised in a barn? You should learn how to show a little restraint. It would be good for you to learn a little decorum instead of rabble rousing in the middle of the day."

I look at her. What do I say to that?

She looks at me. "Well? Do you need something?"

"Oh, uh, yeah. Sorry. We were..." I wave toward my friends, "We were just looking for Emma. Is she still here?"

"Who?"

"'Edna.' We're looking for 'Edna.'"

"Edna bathed Mr. Nutsy for me. It's all sorted out now." She starts to close the door.

"But, wait!" I push the door open. "Is she still here? Where did she go?"

"I'm sure that is none of your concern."

"But it is. We can't find her. Did she tell you where she was going?"

"Edna knows her duty. She's a good girl. Now run along back to the picnic. I have pie." And she closes the door with a thud and a click of the latch.

"Dude. That was useless."

"I guess she's not here," Ann says.

"Why would she hang out any longer than she had to anyway?" I say.

"Maybe if there were cookies." Bean says. "Or pie?"

I look at Bean and Ann and we all shrug.

"What now?" Ann asks.

I look back at the door. "I don't know. But something doesn't seem right."

Ann looks around and then says, "You know? I think we should pray."

Pray? Like out loud?

Bean and I look at each other, then at our shoes.

"Dear Lord…"

She means out loud.

"Please help us find Emma. She's my best friend. Something tells me she's in trouble. Take care of her. Amen."

Silence. Ann elbows me. My turn, I guess. "Um, Lord, I know that you, like, know everything, so I guess you know where Emma is right now."

Yeah, just like he knows where my mom is?

"So, could you, um, show us where she is?"

And my mom, too?

"Amen."

Bean clears his throat, "Amen."

Dude, wish I'd thought of that.

I look over at Mrs. Holmes's porch. "Do you think we should tell the sheriff?"

"Maybe we should," Bean says.

"Wait, let's just look around first. I mean, right now we don't really have anything to tell her. We need some kind of clue or something."

We walk around the house, peering into windows. It's hard to see through the drapes, but we get little glimpses of furniture. No people.

"What about down there?" Ann points at the basement window.

I get down on my knees and peer in. The window's dirty so I rub some of the grime off with my hand and look again.

Emma's down there! I can't see well. I can't tell if she's OK. She's sitting in a chair with her back to the window. She isn't moving. Just sitting.

Why would she be in the basement? And why did Mrs. Holmes lie?

"She's in there," I whisper.

I tap on the window and Emma turns her head.

"Who's in there?" I jump. Mrs. Holmes

stands over us carrying a shovel.

My heart bounces around in my chest. Ann screams. We all jump up and run, but Bean trips. "Save yourselves!" he says. "Run!"

I stop and look back. I mean, this is Mrs. Holmes here. Innocent crazy lady. I walk back to Bean.

But then... I glance toward the window, maybe she's not so innocent.

"Why is she in your basement?" I say.

"Why are you nosing around? It's my business whom I invite into my home young man. I don't like impertinence." She sticks the shovel in the ground and starts digging a hole.

"Going to put those plants in the ground. Maybe the Boogonians will leave them alone then."

"But..."

"Don't interrupt me, you hear me? Now you kids run along. Don't come creeping around again. Now go."

We all look at each other. I guess it's time to get help.

20

We race into the park, looking for Loretta. I don't see her anywhere, but I find my dad leaning against a tree with his eyes closed.

"Where's Loretta?" I say, putting my hands on my knees to catch some breath.

"Dagnabit, don't sneak up on me like that."

"I need to find Loretta."

"I reckon she's with The Old Guy Who Lives in the Park."

I look around. "Where? I thought he was

sick."

"She told me that he's getting out of the hospital today. They're moving him into the nursing home."

"Dad, Mrs. Holmes has Emma in her basement."

He just looks at me. "So?"

"I don't know. It just seems weird."

"You know her. She's always doing something weird, ain't she? Now, let me finish my nap."

"But Dad…"

He shoos me away. Dang it. He's not going to take me seriously. What am I supposed to do?

Maybe if Loretta is at the nursing Home….

I yell for Bean who has been distracted by a juggler. "Come on."

Ann sees us and comes too. "Where we

going? Did you find the sheriff?"

"Nah, but I might know where she is."

"You know, she's probably just got Emma doing some other chore down there. We're kinda overreacting, don't you think?" Beans says.

"I don't know, dude, it just feels wrong."

We run the two blocks to the nursing home and I rush in the front door. A nurse stands there with her arms full of blankets and gives me a look.

"Is the sheriff here?"

"No. She's supposed to be bringing in a patient, but she's not here yet."

I rush back outside.

"Dudes, she isn't here. Maybe we should just go in there ourselves."

"In her basement?" Ann says.

"Yeah. I mean, what else can we do? Emma is in there. And I don't think she wants to be. And...

what if..."

What if she has my mom, too? Could Mom really have been locked in that basement all this time? My hands start shaking and I walk toward Mrs. Holmes' house.

We luck out. When we get to Mrs. Holmes' house we see her walking away. Back straight, ivory-handled walking stick swinging around in ridiculous arcs, and a plant in one hand. Must be taking it for a walk.

We rush through the gate and around to the basement window. Maybe Emma has already gone.

Nope. She's still there, sitting the exact same way.

I push against the window, but it won't budge. I knock. Emma's head turns but not far enough that I can see her eyes. She doesn't move anything else. That's weird.

"Let's try the door."

The door is locked. Of course. But it was worth a try.

"Let's spread out. Try all the windows. I'll go this way." I run around a corner while Ann and Bean go the other direction.

Each window I try is locked tight. I've got to get her out of there.

Why would Mrs. Holmes have her anyway?

I look at the fresh earth around the newly planted flower.

Boogonians.

"Bean!"

He and Ann come from the front of the house,

"Remember when Mrs. Holmes talked about Steve in her basement?" I say.

"No."

"Dude, she had Steve in her basement. We thought it was a plant. Now she has "Edna" in her basement, too."

Ann is on her knees looking in at Emma.

Bean nods, "Yeah, so? Isn't Steve a plant?"

"I think she has Stan down there."

We run around back and that door is open. Only a latched screen door stands in the way. I'm sure I can break it down. That's like, illegal, though, isn't it? I pull on the door, testing how secure it is.

A noise inside distracts me. That stupid monkey. He just sits there on the kitchen table grinning.

"Come here, Nutsy. Open the door."

He just grins.

"I've got peanuts."

Nutsy hops off the table and drags a stool over to the door, climbs up and lifts the hook out of the eye. Dude. Now I wish I had some peanuts.

"We're in!" I say.

"Far out!"

I slip into the house and Nutsy climbs up my leg and begins searching all my pockets. I stand like a statue. I'm not scared or anything, but dang, I hate that monkey.

Sweat is breaking out on my forehead. "Peanuts. Peanuts. Got any peanuts?" I look at Ann and Bean.

"Sure." Bean sticks his hand in a pocket and pulls out a package of Corn Nuts and then shoves them back in and digs into another pocket. After extracting several snacks, he finally produces a bag of peanuts and tosses them to me. They fall on the floor because I can't seem to move.

"Now aren't you glad I wear cargo pants, man?" Bean grins. I'm always giving him a hard time for not wearing jeans like everyone else.

As Mr. Nutsy leaps off me I shiver. Creepy monkey.

There's a door right there in the kitchen that's locked with a slide lock. I unlock it and open the door. Stairs to the basement.

I motion for Bean and Ann.

"Emma?" I say toward the stairs.

No answer.

We creep down, each stair squealing in protest to our steps.

A crash makes us all jump and look upstairs.

"Bean, you'd better be lookout."

He nods and returns to the kitchen.

"It was just the monkey," he whispers loudly.

It's mostly dark in the basement, but Emma

is sitting in light from the window. Her eyes widen as she sees us. Her mouth has a rag tied around it. Ann and I rush over and untie her.

"I'm so glad you came." Her eyes are red and swollen. "I was so scared."

"Why did she do this?"

"She's crazy! She kept talking about Boogonians and said I was in league with him." She points to a dark corner.

I reach over my head and pull the chain connected to the light bulb.

Stan.

There he is tied to a chair and gagged. The chair is chained to a pipe. His eyes are wide and he's squirming as much as he can.

I look around. "Mom?"

She's not here. I thought for sure that when I found Stan...

"Dude!" I go over and take the gag off Stan. "Where's my mom?"

"Get me out of here. Get me away from that mad-woman." His eyes are wild and his greasy hair is sticking out all over the place. I used to be scared of him. Now he just looks flabby and... small.

21

Emma, Ann, and I work at the ropes tying Stan's hands. These knots are tougher than the ones Emma had. He's been pulling on them.

"Come on, come on…" Stan says.

"We're trying. Is there a knife down here anywhere?"

"She took my pocket knife, it might be over on that table." He points with a nod.

Ann rummages around through the junk on the table. "Don't see it."

"Bean, bring down a knife."

I hear him rustling through drawers and then he comes down and tosses a steak knife at my feet. I start sawing on the ropes and Bean pulls a pocket knife out of one of his pockets and helps.

"Dude, where's my mom?" I say again.

"What?"

"My mom. My mom. Lily MacGillicudy." I stop cutting and stare him right in his mean ol' snake eyes. "I know you know where she is. What did you do with her?" I hold the knife up, trying to look threatening.

A door closes and there are footsteps in the living room.

Shoot, shoot, shoot, shoot, shoot...

Stan pulls against the weakened ropes, popping them loose. I drop the knife and it slides under the furnace.

Bean runs up the stairs and pulls the basement door closed. "She's coming!"

We all look around. Can we hide? Can we fit through the window?

She's in the kitchen now. "Where did these peanuts come from, Mr. Nutsy?"

"Oh my gosh!" Ann and Emma are nearly crying.

Stan is trying to get the knife.

Finally I say, "Dudes. It's an old lady."

"A crazy old lady," Stan says. "And she's stronger than she seems." His face is white and his eyes big and crazy looking.

The doorknob turns, "Why isn't this locked? Have you been a naughty monkey?"

The door opens, "Steve? Edna?"

"There's five of us and one of her. Let's just go up there and walk out the door."

They all nod and we move toward the stairs, everyone pushing to be last. "You're forgetting about the monkey," Stan mutters.

I get shoved to the front and start up the steps. Shoot. The noise. No point in sneaking. She'll hear every step. I barrel up in a mad dash, shoving her aside at the top.

"Mark! What in the world…?"

I rush past and out the back door, hoping everyone else is following me. They all stumble out the door onto the lawn and then Mrs. Holmes screeches at us through the screen. "No. You can't go. You can't. It's not safe. There will be no stopping the Boogonians now."

We all scurry through the gate and onto the sidewalk. Just then we see Loretta exiting the nursing home and we run, each of us yelling our own version of what's going on.

Loretta looks at us like we're a herd of hippos or something. Then she sees Stan and her expression changes to look like we're zebra-striped hippos.

I pull on Loretta's sleeve, "Make him tell you where Mom is."

She turns to me, "What?"

"He won't tell me..." I say.

"That crazy woman..." Stan says.

"...made me wash her monkey and..." Emma says.

"...there was a shovel and something about Boogonians...." Ann says.

"...I found some peanuts to distract..." Bean says.

"Everybody shut up!" Loretta hollers.

She turns back to me. "What about your mom?"

"He knows where she is. He did something to her. Make him tell you what he did. Take him downtown. Shine that light in his face and stuff." I glare at Stan. He used to scare me, but now he just makes me mad. "Make him tell you."

My voice is shaking, but I don't care. "He knows where she is."

"All right, Match, calm down." She looks us over. "One at a time. What's going on?"

Everyone starts in again.

"Stan. You tell me. Everyone else, hush."

"That crazy old lady had me locked in her basement."

Loretta's eyes widen.

Emma butts in, "She made me wash her monkey, then she tied me up in her basement, too."

"You? When did that happen?" Loretta asks.

"This afternoon."

Loretta looks across the road at Mrs. Holmes and sighs, then she looks at Stan. "Now, you're not under arrest or anything, but can you come to my office and answer some questions?"

"Make him tell you about my mom!"

"I don't know what this kid's talking about. But I'll come down and do whatever you need. I sure as heck want that crazy bat arrested."

"But, Loretta…"

"Match, I'll take care of this. You kids get back to the picnic. I may need to talk to you later. I'll let you know."

Dude. She acts like she doesn't even care about Mom.

She puts her hand on my shoulder. "If he knows anything, I'll find out. I miss her, too, you know." She looks over my shoulder and shakes her head. "But first, I've got to go arrest an old lady."

I turn and look at Mrs. Holmes crying in her yard.

22

Dad made me go home with him after the fireworks were over. Said I couldn't go to Loretta's house and harass her. So this morning after he makes me do chores I ride my bike to her office.

It isn't open yet, so I wait on the steps.

She waves when she pulls into her parking spot and then comes and sits on the steps with me.

"That was quite the adventure you had yesterday, Match."

"So, what did he say about Mom? Did you go

get her yet?"

She puts her arm around my shoulders. Oh oh. That can't be good. I shrug it off, stand up and move down to the sidewalk.

"He doesn't know anything about where your mom is, Match."

"But…"

She cuts me off. "Why do you think he would?"

"Well…these old guys said…"

"What did they say?"

I swallow hard. "Nothing, I guess."

"If they said something that I need to know…" She puts her hand on my arm.

I shrug away. "They didn't, all right."

"You need to tell me what you know so I can help your mom."

"They said she ran off with Stan. Does that

help?" I glare at her.

"Oh honey. I promise you that didn't happen."

Honey? Gag.

"How do you know? Maybe she ran off to be with him before Mrs. Holmes kidnapped him."

"Seriously? You really think your mom would choose to be with Stan? Really? Come on. She didn't like him any more than anyone else."

She's got a point.

"I'm sorry, Match, but we just don't know where she is."

I just need to know something. Anything.

"Well, maybe she didn't run off with him. Maybe he kidnapped her. Maybe if you stopped eating Snickers long enough to do your job you'd actually find her." I run outside and peel out of there on my bike. Tears blur my vision. Stupid

Loretta. Stupid Stan. Stupid, stupid….

Stupid Mom.

A couple of blocks away I see Stan on the corner, chewing on sunflower seeds. I pull my bike up next to him. I want to get off and pound him in the chest, but I don't think that's mature.

"Loretta said you don't know anything about my mom. You need to tell me, dude. She's my mom."

"You saved me from that crazy lady and I really appreciate that." He spits sunflower shells onto the street. "It chaps my hide to be rescued by a kid. It's bad enough to be tied up by an old lady."

"How'd she do that anyway? You're way bigger than her."

"She had me in there fixin' her pipes. She told me to sit down and eat a cookie and have some lemonade. She's kinda hard to say no to."

I grunt in agreement.

"So I did. I guess she had some sleeping pills in the lemonade or something. I woke up tied to the chair."

"Dude." Think of all the times I've had her lemonade. "Well, anyway, you gotta tell me about my mom."

"Kid, I can't. I don't know anything." The way he looks at me, I know he's telling the truth.

I can feel my eyes stinging. The last thing I need is to cry in front of this guy. If he doesn't know something, then who does?

He wads up the sunflower seed bag and tosses it onto the sidewalk. "Sorry, kid." Then he walks away.

◆ ◆ ◆

On Saturday, Dad walks into the house with a handful of mail. His face is pale and he doesn't look at me. "There's something for you here."

He just stands there at the table with his back to me.

"Ok. Who's it from?"

No answer.

"Can you toss it here?"

Nothing.

"Dad?"

He turns around, his eyes are damp, and he holds out a letter.

I get up off the couch and walk over to take it. He's holding it so tightly that I have to tug to get it away.

What's going on?

I look down to see who it's from but there's

no return address. My name and address are written in familiar handwriting. I rush to my room and get my wallet and take out the folded note. I've seen this writing a thousand times: "I love you, honey! Have a good day." Notes in my lunchbox, under my pillow, on the bathroom mirror. This note was in my backpack. I don't know how long it was there. I found it a week after she disappeared.

I close the door. The postmark says New York. Dude, what's she doing there?

I rip the envelope and pull out the single sheet of paper.

> Matty,
>
> I just wanted to let
> you know that I'm all
> right. I'm so sorry if
> you've been worried about

me. I had no intention of hurting you, yet I know that I have.

I wish I could explain why I left, but I can't right now. I don't even know how. But I want you to know that I love you. You have no idea how much. My leaving had absolutely nothing to do with you. Please believe me.

I miss you and I think of you every minute. Every single minute.

Love, love, love you.

Mom

I turn the paper over. That's it?

My eyes sting. I lay face down on the bed and bury my face in a pillow. I'm not crying, though. Not over this. Not over her. I crumple the paper and hold it in my fist.

Thanks for nothing, Mom. No explanation. No return address. Nothing.

After awhile I sit up and look out the window. At least I know she's alive, though. And maybe, if she really misses me like she said, maybe she'll, like, come home, you know?

I smooth out the crumpled letter and put it on my desk.

23

Bean and I are sitting on a downed tree in the middle of the circle. The weird smell has gone. But there's something different about this place from anywhere else.

"What's up, man? You're acting funky."

Bean had been bugging me all the way up the trail. He isn't going to let up. I need to learn how to hide my feelings better. Or else I should have come alone. I wanted to. But I didn't want to be alone. Know what I mean?

"C'mon Match. Let's have it."

I look up at the sky. "Got a letter from Mom."

"WHAT? No way!" He jumps up and comes over to stand in front of me balancing on a log lower than the one I'm on. "She's alive? Man, that is far out. Where is she? Is she coming home? Can she…."

"Dude."

"Sorry. But, man!"

"The postmark's from New York."

"What's she doin' there?"

"I don't know." I pick at the bark on the tree. Peeling it off layer by layer. "All she said was that she's all right, she loves me, and she misses me."

I get up and scramble over the logs to get to regular ground.

"Man, that's a drag. But at least you know that she isn't dead or anything."

I stop and look at him. "Yeah. I'm glad she isn't dead. But... you know, a person can't help dying."

"What's that mean?"

"Dude. She *chose* to leave. It was her decision. She wanted to go."

"Seems like she always loved you a lot. It was kinda cool, you know, the way she acted around you. I bet she still feels the same way."

I just shrug.

◆ ◆ ◆

When I get home, Dad is cleaning the tack in the yard.

He waves me over. "Come help me out."

Oh brother. I scuff on over there and grab a rag and start wiping down a saddle.

"I got a letter, too," he says.

"Really? What'd it say?" I shield my eyes to look at him.

"Nothing really. She said she's sorry."

"Did she say when she'll be home or tell you why she left?"

"Nope."

Dang it.

"Listen," he says. "I should have been talking to you about her all this time. Truth is, I'm lost without her. I didn't know what to do."

He lifts his hat to wipe sweat away and then looks at me.

"Point is, I'm sorry. I was wrong to leave you in the dark. I was wrong to not consider how it was affecting you. Shoot sometimes I still think you should be four years old instead of fourteen. I forget that you're old enough to talk to about this stuff."

He reaches over and puts his hand on my head. "We OK? You forgive me?"

I shrug. Dude, that's a lot to take in. I don't think he's ever apologized to me before.

He picks up a saddle and walks toward the barn.

"Dad?"

He turns and looks at me.

"Yeah. We're OK."

❖ ❖ ❖

"Hey there," Loretta says. "I heard about your mom."

I stopped in to get the latest on Mrs. Holmes.

She opens her desk drawer, "Want a Snickers?"

She pulls out two and hands one to me.

"You bet. Thanks!" I plop into the chair opposite her.

I guess she's given up the sneaking? Or maybe she's started sneaking something else. I look at her suspiciously. Yep. I bet she's found a new vice. She likes sneaky.

She smiles at me as though she's reading my thoughts.

"So, Loretta, what did you get out of Mrs. Holmes? Why'd she kidnap those guys?

"Because she's crazy, Match. That's why."

"Yeah, but what'd she tell you?"

She sighs and leans her chair back.

"She talked a lot about plants and some creatures, aliens, she said, called Boogonians. Apparently they come to earth to steal our plants. She thinks it's a plot to deprive us of oxygen. Stan was in league with these Boogonians, according to her. He was contacting them and giving them tactical information."

"Dude. But what about Emma?"

"I guess Mr. Nutsy informed Mrs. Holmes that Emma had told him Boogonian secrets while she was bathing him. Obviously, she was in cahoots, too."

I laugh and shake my head. "That is like, so nuts!"

"Yeah. We've got her living in the nursing home now. They even let her have her monkey." I give her a look, because she knows how I feel about that monkey.

She shrugs. "The assisted living part allows pets." She peels some chocolate off the outside of the candy bar and puts it in her mouth. "The doctors are trying some medication and apparently she has some vitamin deficiencies and what-not. They think she'll improve with better nutrition. She lived on hot dogs and cupcakes. That's it. I don't know how she stayed so thin. But, apparently, a brain gets pretty deprived on a diet like that."

"I would think so."

"And uh, what about you?" I ask.

"What do you mean?"

"You know, that trouble you were in?"

"Oh that." She talks around a big mouth full of Snickers. "He decided not to press charges. He actually seems like he's mellowed out a little bit. Maybe this experience was good for him."

"Good for us, you mean. That is, if it lasts."

◆ ◆ ◆

Mr. Mac has been feeling a lot better, so I'm going to see him for the first time since everything went down.

"Hey, Matt," Liz says. "I hear you're a hero."

My cheeks get warm and I look at my shoes.

"Found Stan. Rescued the girl. Sounds pretty heroic to me." She's smiling all big.

"Guess so."

She puts a hand on my arm. "I'm glad you heard from your mom. My guess is that you'll hear from her a lot more now."

"You think so?"

"Yes. I do. I think making the first contact was the hardest. It will be easier for her to write now."

"I hope so."

I turn toward Mr. Mac's room and almost fall down. Before I get there The Old Guy Who Lives in the Park stops me.

"Match," he puts a hand on my shoulder. "I want to thank you."

"For what?"

He gestures to a couple of chairs, "Can you sit for a minute?"

"All right."

We sit and he pulls his chair closer to mine, looks intently at my face.

"You know I really didn't want to come here."

I nod.

"I loved living out there in the park. Loved the freedom." He looks out the window next to us.

I watch him. Wondering if our conversation is over. When he looks back at me, his eyes are wet.

"I know who I am."

I smile and nod. Is this guy losing it?

"No, Match, I mean, I know *who* I am."

24

"What do you mean, you know who you are?" I ask The Old Guy. "You got your memory back?"

"I was sitting here looking out the window just like this one day when I saw some people walking up the front walk. It was a tall beautiful woman and the sheriff. Something drew me to them so I walked out onto the front steps.

The woman looked up at me, her face broke into a smile and she said, 'Mark! It's you.'

And I knew. Right in that moment it all came

back to me. My name is Mark Holmes. Deborah is my wife. I was a pilot."

"Wait. Craz...I mean, Mrs. Holmes is your *wife*?"

He smiled at me. "Yes, she is."

"How did you forget?"

"I was in a plane crash. The only memory I had was of waking up in the park one morning. Apparently I had made my way here from the crash site. I remember that I had a terrible headache for days. Probably a concussion. And I remember that I was in pretty bad shape. They didn't suspect I was from the crash, because it was miles away. They didn't think anyone had survived. I guess the whole thing burned up after I got out."

"Dude. That's pretty awesome."

He grins.

"But why didn't anyone recognize you? If your wife lived here, wouldn't people know who you were?"

"No. We lived in Denver at the time. We were planning to move up here because Deborah's sister gave us that house. I crashed before we finished packing. Deborah moved on her own."

"Wow. That's pretty weird. How do these things happen? I mean, dude."

"There's a lot of things that can't be explained. We just accept them."

Hmm.

He puts his hand on my shoulder. "So I wanted to thank you for helping my love come to this place. I would never have found her otherwise." A tear slips over his bottom lid. "Just two blocks apart all these years. I wouldn't leave the park and she wouldn't come north." He shakes his head.

"But I can't spend my days in regret." He says. "We're together now and I'm going to enjoy every moment." He pats my shoulder and then stands up. "Time for us to have tea. It's one of our traditions."

I watch him walk away, amazed by his story. Who would'a ever guessed?

Old Guy gets to see his wife again. Mr. Mac has Stan back. I wonder when I'll get to see Mom again.

◆ ◆ ◆

Mr. Mac is sitting in his chair reading a book.

"Hi, Mr. Mac. How you feeling?"

He looks up and grins. His teeth are in a glass by his bed. "I'M DOIN' REAL GOOD, LITTLE

MAC. REAL GOOD" He moves some newspapers off his bed. "HERE, TAKE A LOAD OFF."

I take a seat and look at him. He looks better, that's for sure. And he sounds better, too. Guess I'll have to start bringing those earplugs again.

"THANK YOU FOR FINDING MY BOY." He grabs my hand in both of his. "YOU SAID YOU WOULD AND I KNEW YOU'D DO IT, TOO ."

"Well, I didn't know I'd do it. I really kinda got lucky, you know?"

"WHATEVER IT WAS, I'M GRATEFUL." He stands up. "HEY, WANT TO GO FOR A WALK?"

I nod and he digs in his pocket and hands me a butterscotch candy.

◆ ◆ ◆

Bean and I are sitting outside Milky Way eating

some ice cream. Ann and Emma come up and sit at our table.

My hands start sweating. I haven't seen her since the big rescue. Her parents took her home right after that.

Bean grins and offers to buy Ann an ice cream. Dude, he's such a dork, yet he's all cool with girls. I don't get it.

I ask Emma if she wants some ice cream.

"No thanks. I just had a Popsicle."

That doesn't make sense, but whatever.

"Maybe it's not my business, but Ann said that you heard from your mom." She says.

Geez, I guess Bean can't keep anything to himself around Ann. Not that it was really a secret, I guess.

I nod.

"That's great, Match."

I look at her. "Really? She's still gone."

"Still, it's really good news." She looks down at her hand.

Dude. I'm such a dope. "I...uh...I forgot that your dad died. I'm sorry."

"No, it's OK." She smiles. "Really."

We watch Bean and Ann take their ice cream to another table. Shoot. I was hoping they'd come back and I wouldn't have to talk anymore.

"I guess it's kinda hard to understand why your mom left, huh? I mean, my dad didn't choose to leave, but your mom.... I mean, I, uh...."

She looks embarrassed, but I'm glad she gets it.

"Yeah, it's OK. I think about that all the time." My eyes are not going to water. Not here. Not now.

"It's not your fault she left, you know?"

I look at her. Why does everyone keep saying that? Like, is it painted on my forehead or something?

"Grown ups have their own stuff we don't know about." She says.

I nod.

"I know what it's like to have questions, though. When my dad died, it drove me crazy wondering why it happened. My mom said that was normal and she felt the same way. But she said God knows the answers to all our 'whys' and thinking about that helped her. I try to think about it, too. It does seem to help sometimes."

She touches my hand with two fingers. All I can think about are those fingers. So soft....

She pulls them away and says, "You know, you'll probably find out what's going on with your mom sooner or later. I mean, she may write again, or maybe you guys can find her now that you have a lead. Something like that?"

"Yeah, you're probably right." I hope so.

Wow. We had a whole conversation and I hardly had to talk at all.

◆ ◆ ◆

I'm eating lunch when I hear a racket outside. I go see what's up. Dad comes out of the barn and Ron and Ray are riding into the yard fast. They had borrowed the horses for some kind of excursion.

"You won't believe it" Ron reins in his horse and jumps off.

Ray is right behind him, leaving the horses to nibble on the lawn.

"Circles...."

"You know those crop circle things...."

"And they're trees! Really. Trees!"

"I never saw anything like it!"

Oh oh. I guess our secret won't be a secret much longer. No way these guys will keep this to themselves. I mean, look at them. They're, like, idiotic with excitement.

Dad is trying to piece together all their jumbled talking. I just stand and watch. I guess when the news gets out, maybe some experts can tell us what the circles are. But I won't hold my breath.

In fact, I've decided maybe I kinda like not knowing.

Things to think about:

1. I am very interested in crop circles. Even though scientists believe people create them, I like to think about other possibilities. Match never learns what caused the tree circles. What are some possible explanations? Is there any realistic explanation for what happened to the trees?

2. Match has a big problem – wondering what happened to his mom. Have you ever had something big like that happen in you life? Something that was hurtful, but also filled you with questions? How did you handle it?

3. Do you believe in God? Match does, and I do. When questions are too big for me, I find comfort knowing that God knows the answers even if I never do. What brings you comfort in

times like that?

4. Sometimes our questions get answered and sometimes they don't. What do you think is the best thing to do when it seems like you're never going to find out what you really want to know? Do you think it's possible to learn to have peace even without answers?

5. The Old Guy can't remember who he is. If that happened to you, what kind of person do you think you might become?

6. Mrs. Holmes and The Old Guy both let fear keep them from living a full life. Do you have fears that get in the way of your life? What might you be missing out on?

7. Do you think the Boogonians really exist in the story or is Mrs. Holmes imagining them?

I'm so glad you read my book. Thank you! I hope you enjoyed it. If you'd like to, you can leave a review on Amazon or Goodreads. You could also tell your friends about it. That would be the best compliment of all.

If you would like to contact me at iamkayday@gmail.com

I want to thank all the people who helped me on this long book-writing journey.

Brent, the kids (who don't want their names mentioned), Mom and Dad, Julie Bradford, Robbie Iobst, Loretta Oakes, Michele Cushatt, Chris Dellacroce, Kim Millsap, Crystal Theringer, Sharen Watson, Denise Holmes, Nancy Rue, Kathy Mackel, Angie Hunt, Bill Myers, members of the Words for the Journey Christian Writers' Guild, and the Glen Eyrie Writers' Workshop.

I truly could not have done it without you. Thank you so much for your help, encouragement, and friendship

Made in the USA
San Bernardino, CA
25 November 2015